RYDER – GONE TO HELL

First published in eBook and paperback 2025

© Wyatt Steele

Wyatt Steele

The right of Wyatt Steele to be identified as the author of this work has been asserted by her in accordance with the Copyright, Designs and Patents Act 1988.

All rights reserved. No part of this publication may be reproduced, stored in or introduced into a retrieval system, or transmitted, in any form, or by any means (electronic, mechanical, photocopying, recording or otherwise) without the prior written permission of the writer. Any person who does any unauthorized act in relation to this publication may be liable to criminal prosecution and civil claims for damages.

Thank you for respecting the hard work of this author.

ALSO BY WYATT STEELE

TRAIL OF THE GUNFIGHTER SERIES

VENDETTA RIDE – THE WRATH OF WYATT EARP

THE OUTLAW McCOY SERIES

DRIFTER GRITTY WESTERN SERIES

Wyatt Steele

Ryder – Gone To Hell

Contents

Introduction 7
Chapter 1 – Wells - Two Weeks Ago 9
Chapter 2 – A Rope for Finn Crowe...........21
Chapter 3 – The Shootout & Escape 30
Chapter 4 – The Posse Rides.....................41
Chapter 5 – A Bad Trail to Follow 51
Chapter 6 – An Ambush in the Rocks........61
Chapter 7 – A Snake in the Posse.............72
Chapter 8 – The Night Before 82
Chapter 9 – The Seeds of Doubt 93
Chapter 10 – A Desperate Gamble..........102
Chapter 11 – A Tense March....................121
Chapter 12 – The Trail Changes...............139
Chapter 13 – The Price of Bad Choices ..147
Chapter 14 - Death Brings Doubt.............162
Chapter 15 - A Dangerous Debate 173
Chapter 16- Bullets in the Dust................188
Chapter 17 – Into Hell 200
Chapter 18 – The Showdown 212
EPILOGUE...220

Wyatt Steele

Ryder – Gone To Hell

Introduction

Gunfire shattered the stillness of the desert dawn. Ryder's heart pounded as he pressed his back against the rough surface of a boulder, the acrid scent of gunpowder filling his nostrils. Bullets whizzed past, ricocheting off rocks and kicking up spurts of sand.

"We're pinned down!" Rourke's voice was strained, a crimson stain spreading across his shoulder.

Ryder risked a glance around the edge of his cover. Madsen's men were entrenched among the ruins ahead, their muzzle flashes lighting up the shadows. The trading post, once a modest sanctuary amidst the desolation, now lay in shambles, its wooden beams splintered and charred.

"Tom, cover fire!" Ryder barked. "Nathan, flank left!"

Tom nodded, his hands steady as he reloaded, then popped up to unleash a volley of shots. Nathan, crouching low, darted toward a cluster of rocks on the left, his movements swift despite the chaos enveloping them.

Ryder felt a presence beside him and turned to see Texas, his face smeared with dirt and sweat, eyes sharp. "Got any bright ideas, cowboy?"

Wyatt Steele

"Yeah," Ryder replied, a grim smile tugging at his lips. "Don't get shot."

Texas chuckled, the sound incongruous amidst the cacophony of battle. "Solid plan."

A sudden cry drew Ryder's attention. He saw Nathan stumble, clutching his leg, blood seeping between his fingers. Anger flared within him. They had to end this, and soon.

Drawing a deep breath, Ryder signaled to Texas. "On my mark, we push forward."

Texas nodded, gripping his rifle tighter.

"Now!"

They surged from cover, firing as they advanced. The distance to the trading post felt endless, each step a battle against the hail of bullets. But determination fueled their charge.

Would they make it?

Ryder – Gone To Hell
Chapter 1 – Wells Crossing - Two Weeks Ago

The wind carried dust down the main street of Wells Crossing, swirling it in idle circles before settling on the smooth, well-swept boardwalks. The town had the look of a place still holding its own, a rare sight along the trails Ryder had been riding. The storefronts weren't sagging, their paint might have been faded by the sun, but the buildings stood solid, well-kept, and used.

    He sat easy in the saddle, the brim of his hat pulled low against the afternoon glare. His buckskin mare, Sparks, moved at a steady gait, hooves muffled by the firm, well-packed road. This place wasn't the kind of dust-choked nothing-town he was used to—there was money here, or at least enough to keep things running.

    Ahead, a sign swung lazily on iron chains, well-oiled so it didn't creak—The Silver Star Saloon. Beneath it, a man in a clean apron leaned against a post, chewing tobacco and spitting into a neat little patch of dirt by his feet. He looked at Ryder like any man would at a stranger, but there was no hunger, no hostility, no warning in his eyes.

Wyatt Steele

That, more than anything, set Ryder on edge.

He guided Sparks to the hitching post, looped her reins over the rail, and gave her a solid pat on the neck before stepping up onto the boardwalk. His spurs jingled lightly against the well-maintained planks. The saloon doors swung inward at his touch, revealing a space that wasn't just surviving but thriving.

Inside, the air smelled of spiced tobacco, polished wood, and whiskey that wasn't the bottom of the barrel. Light streamed through clean windows, catching the rich, dark wood of a long, sturdy bar. The floors were swept, the poker tables were solid and level, and the piano had a cloth covering it to keep the dust off.

A good saloon in a small town. That was rare enough to be worth noting.

Behind the bar, a broad-shouldered man with a salt-and-pepper beard and a steady gaze set down a glass he'd been drying. He looked Ryder up and down—not unfriendly, not nervous, just taking stock.

"Howdy, cowboy?" he said, his voice as easy as the slow afternoon. "What'll it be?"

"Whiskey," Ryder said, fishing a coin from his vest pocket.

The bartender poured a measure into a clean, unchipped glass and slid it across the bar. Ryder lifted it, took a slow sip, and paused.

Ryder – Gone To Hell

It was good.

Not just *not bad*, not just *drinkable*—but actually good.

The shock must have shown on his face because the bartender let out a short huff of a laugh.

"Name's Texas Bill—most folks just call me Texas," he said, reaching for another glass. "If I don't like it, I don't serve it. Saloon might be a little beat-up around the edges, but the whiskey's good, company usually is, and my Lila Jay cooks some damn fine food."

Ryder leaned an elbow on the bar and gave the place another look. The details added up.

The tables and chairs were sturdy, the bar well-kept. The floor had been swept, not just kicked clean. Even the mirrors behind the counter were polished enough to catch the lamplight. The place told a story—somewhere along the way, someone had built this saloon to last. The man stepped off the porch, boots scuffing against the wooden boards.

"What's your name, stranger?"

Ryder adjusted his hat, dusted off his coat, and met Texas's gaze. "Ryder."

Texas smirked, his eyes running over Ryder from head to toe. "Just Ryder?"

Ryder let the question hang between them a beat. Then, he nodded once. "Yeah. Just Ryder."

Wyatt Steele

Texas chuckled. "That right?"

"That's right." Texas's eyes shifted back to the saloon, "It's quiet now," Texas Bill continued, pouring himself a finger of whiskey. "But give it another couple hours, the hands'll start drifting in. We do good business here. You're in the right place, cowboy."

Ryder couldn't quite remember the last time he'd ridden into a town like this. A place where the saloon wasn't full of hopeless men drinking their last dime, waiting for a bullet. He picked up his glass and took another sip.

"Got rooms," Texas said, watching him. "Two bits a night. If you want one out back where it's quieter, that'll cost you a little extra. You want to see 'em?"

Ryder set his glass down and glanced toward the stairwell.

A good saloon, good whiskey, good rooms. That was enough to make a man cautious. Still, maybe for once, he'd found a place worth stopping in.

Ryder lifted his glass and drained the last of the whiskey. It left a slow burn down his throat, smooth enough that he figured Texas Bill had been telling the truth—he didn't serve anything he wouldn't drink himself. When Ryder set the glass down, Texas was already watching him, one hand resting on the bar, the other wiping a clean rag along the counter.

Ryder – Gone To Hell

"You want to take a look at them rooms?" Texas asked.

Ryder gave a slight nod.

Texas tossed the rag onto the bar and stepped out from behind the counter, stretching his back as he did. "Alright then. Follow me."

He led Ryder across the saloon and up a narrow flight of stairs, the boards creaking under their boots but solid beneath the weight. No rot, no sagging. The rail had been polished smooth by years of hands gripping it, and the hallway above was well-lit by a single oil lamp fixed to the wall.

Texas motioned to the first door, pushing it open without a key. "Got a couple rooms at the front," he said, stepping aside so Ryder could see.

Ryder leaned in. It smelled fresh. Not of dust and stale air but of wood and a faint hint of soap. The bed was plain but well-made, the kind of mattress that wouldn't leave a man with a crick in his back. A small nightstand with a glass oil lamp and a single chair tucked into a wooden writing desk. The window faced the street, and through the clean glass, Ryder could see the stagecoach station opposite, a livery beside it, and further on, the dry, stretching road out of town.

"Basic, but clean," Texas said, crossing his arms. "Other rooms face the back. Look out over the desert. Some folk prefer that."

Ryder thought about it. After weeks on the trail, a view of the plains wasn't something he needed.

"I'll take this one," he said.

Texas gave a nod. "Suit yourself. Stage station gets some traffic, but it's not bad. Better than listening to coyotes screaming their guts out all night."

He reached into his vest and pulled out a brass key, tossing it to Ryder, who caught it easily.

"Two bits a night," Texas reminded him. "If you're staying longer, I'll cut you a deal. Pay when you leave."

Ryder slipped the key into his pocket.

"Need a place for your horse?"

"Yeah."

"Willy Scott owns the livery across the way," Texas said, nodding toward the station. "Tell him I sent you, and he'll give you a fair price."

Ryder stepped back into the hall, glancing at the other doors. No sound behind them, no sign of other guests. Quiet, for now.

Texas turned, leading the way back down the stairs. "I keep a good house," he said over his shoulder. "Don't go in for the kind of trouble other places let slide."

Ryder didn't answer, but he didn't doubt it. He stepped out of the saloon and into the evening heat, crossing the street to the livery. The smell of hay, leather, and horse sweat met him as he pushed open the heavy wooden doors. The stable was well-kept, the floors swept down, stalls clean. A farrier's anvil stood near the open doors, tools neatly arranged on a bench.

A wiry old man with a weathered face and silver-streaked beard stepped out of a stall, dusting off his hands. His sharp gray eyes ran over Ryder, then flicked to Sparks, who waited patiently outside.

"That your horse?"

Ryder nodded.

"She looks sound," the man said, spitting to the side. "Ain't seen a buckskin that fine in a while."

"Texas sent me," Ryder said.

The old man—Willy Scott, Ryder presumed—grunted. "That so? Well, he don't send just anyone, so I reckon I can give you a fair price."

He motioned for Ryder to bring Sparks in. Ryder led her into an open stall while Willy grabbed a bucket of water and set it down.

"Got good hay, fresh water. I'll check her hooves in the mornin' if you're stayin' more'n a day," Willy said, giving the horse a once-over. "You need tack cleaned, that'll cost extra."

Wyatt Steele

Ryder pulled a few coins from his pocket and handed them over.

Willy weighed them in his palm, then nodded. "She'll be well cared for."

That was good enough for Ryder.

He stepped out, giving Sparks a final pat before heading back across the street toward the Silver Star.

By the time Ryder stepped back into the Silver Star, the saloon had come alive.

The low hum of conversation had grown into a steady, rolling murmur, punctuated by the clink of glasses and the shuffle of boots. The warm glow of lamplight and tobacco smoke filled the room, curling through the rafters. The piano had been uncovered and a grizzled old player hunched over the keys, picking out a slow, rambling tune, the kind that told stories without words. The crowd had thickened, men gathered at the bar and clustered around poker tables. The dealer worked steady hands, cards flicking across green felt, chips stacking up. The bark of laughter mixed with the occasional grumble of a losing hand.

Ryder let his eyes move over the room, taking in the details. A lively saloon in a thriving town. The kind of place most men could sit and drink without worrying if they'd see sunrise.

Texas Bill caught sight of him and nodded, setting down a glass. "Figured you'd be back," he said, tilting his head toward an empty stool.

Ryder took the seat, setting his hat beside him. "Told me you had good food," he said. "Figured I'd find out."

Texas grinned. "Smart man." He turned toward the back. "Lila! Stew plate for our new friend here."

A sharp and friendly voice answered from the kitchen. "Already working on it."

Lila Jay moved through the saloon with the ease of a woman who'd spent years in places like this and knew exactly how to handle herself. She carried a plate of stew in one hand, the scent of slow-cooked meat and rich gravy trailing behind her, her steps light but sure.

She wasn't a young woman—not anymore—but she was still a good-looking one. The same age as Texas Bill, though the years had been kind to her. The kind of woman who could turn heads without trying, not because she was some fresh-faced girl, but because she had a presence about her. A confidence that made men take notice.

Her chestnut-brown hair had a few lighter strands running through it, sun-kissed from years beneath the open sky. It fell in soft waves over one shoulder, catching the lantern glow like polished wood. Her skin was tanned, smooth in some places, lined in others, but there was something striking about her—sharp cheekbones, a strong jaw, and a mouth quick to smile.

Her eyes, a green too bright for a dusty frontier town, held a sharpness that said she saw more than she let on. A woman who'd learned to read men the way a gambler reads a deck, who could pick out trouble long before it arrived at her door.

When she reached Ryder's table, she set the plate down in front of him with a knowing smile. She looked him up and down, "Didn't realise I was feeding a giant! Texas you shoulda told me! A boy like this needs more an' you do to keep him standing." Then to Ryder she said confidentially, "I'll be right back with something else."

Ryder accepted the plate, smiling. "Thank you ma'am, it'll be plenty."

Ryder seated himself at a table next to the bar where she'd set the plate down. "Busy for a weeknight."

Texas poured himself a drink, then glanced around the saloon like a man who knew every soul in the place. "Folks are in town for the hanging."

Ryder took a sip, waiting.

Texas didn't leave him waiting long.

"Dale Madsen," he said, wiping down the counter in front of him. "You heard of him?"

Ryder shook his head.

Ryder – Gone To Hell

Texas snorted. "Lucky you."

Texas rested his forearms against the bar, lowering his voice just enough to keep it between them. "Man was a damn nightmare. Killed a dozen people that we know of. Ranchers, homesteaders, travelers. Didn't care. Would ride onto a place, take what he wanted, and leave the bodies behind."

Ryder picked up his fork, cutting into the tender beef. "Plenty of men like that," he said, not looking up.

Texas exhaled, shaking his head. "This one was worse."

Ryder took a bite. The stew was good. Real good.

"Last killing he did," Texas went on, voice flat, "was Sally Kittering."

The name didn't mean anything to Ryder, but Texas saw the look on his face and filled in the gaps.

"The wheelwright's daughter. Seventeen. Good girl. She was alone when Madsen and his men rode in. He—" Texas broke off, jaw tightening. "Took her with him."

Ryder set his fork down. He didn't ask for details. He didn't need them. He knew what men like Madsen did to girls like that.

"They found her body two days later," Texas said, voice low. "Sheriff and his men tracked him for three weeks. Caught him on the edge of the territory, running low on men and out of bullets."

Ryder picked up his whiskey. Took a slow drink.

"He'll swing in the morning," Texas finished. "And if there's a hell, he'll be going down with the devil."

Ryder didn't answer right away. He let the weight of it sit between them.

Outside, the wind picked up, rattling the saloon windows. Somewhere down the street, a dog barked.

Chapter 2 – A Rope for Finn Crowe

The smell of hot coffee and crisp bacon met Ryder when he awoke. The town was already awake, voices drifting up from the street below, boots scuffing on the boardwalks, the iron clang of a blacksmith hammering in the distance. He sat up slowly, stretching the stiffness from his shoulders. Outside his window, Wells Crossing was moving early, folk gathering in groups, talking in low voices. He didn't have to ask why.

The hanging.

Ryder ran a hand over his face, then reached for his boots.

Downstairs, the Silver Star was packed. The usual morning quiet of a saloon was gone, replaced with the low murmur of men and women who'd come to see justice done. There were men in their Sunday suits and shirts sitting alongside grim-faced ranchers with fresh-shaven jaws and a handful of travel-worn men who looked like they'd ridden in just for this. A few sat alone, staring into black coffee, lost in thoughts too deep for morning. Others spoke in tight whispers, voices edged with anger or sorrow. The saloon was hot already with body heat, and from the cooking fires out back, the scent of fresh-brewed coffee was thick in the air, mingling with the crisp bite of frying bacon.

Texas Bill was waiting at the bar, already watching Ryder. He jerked his chin toward an empty seat near the corner. "Saved you a table," he said. "Figured you'd be along."

Ryder nodded once, taking the seat. A fresh cup of coffee was already poured. He lifted it and took a slow sip. It was good. Damn good. Lila Jay moved through the room with practiced ease, balancing plates of bacon, eggs, and griddle cakes, setting them down with quick efficiency. The kind of woman who'd been running this kitchen long enough to know exactly what every man in town wanted before they asked. When she reached Ryder, she set down a plate of thick-cut bacon, eggs fried dark around the edges, and cornbread still steaming.

She met his eyes for half a second. "Eat up, Cowboy." Then she was gone, vanishing into the back again.

Ryder took another sip of coffee and let the saloon play out around him. There were men at every table, folk rubbing at tired eyes, hands shaking slightly as they lifted their cups. Some looked angry, their expressions tight, the weight of vengeance sitting heavy on their shoulders. Others had a hollowed-out look; grief settled deep into their bones. All of them were connected by the same man.

Dale Madsen.

Ryder didn't feel much of anything. The law would do its job. That was the end of it, he was far more interested in the bacon and the coffee than the hanging. Texas leaned against the bar, watching him eat. After a while, he said, "You gonna come watch?"

Ryder glanced up, chewing. "I seen hangings before."

Texas gave a short huff. "Ain't like this one. Not often you see a whole town show up to send a man down to hell."

Ryder swallowed and then took another sip of the dark coffee; he really didn't want to join the crowd; this was town business, not his.

Texas watched him, eyes glinting. "Come on, cowboy. It's a short walk. No harm seeing a man take his last breath. And this one deserves the drop, I can tell you."

Ryder sighed. The coffee was too damn good to leave unfinished, but Texas had a look in his eye that said he wouldn't let it go. So Ryder obliged. Outside, the town had gathered in the square. The gallows stood across from the Silver Star, a sturdy thing, freshly built—like the folk of Wells Crossing had planned to use it more than once. A thick crowd had gathered, near a

Wyatt Steele

hundred strong. Men, women, and quite a few children held tight to their fathers' hands. From his spot near the saloon doors, Ryder watched without much interest. The morning sun was climbing, casting long shadows across the dirt street. People shifted on their feet, waiting. Whoever Dale Madsen was, he'd sure as hell pissed off a lot of folks.

The jailhouse door opened. Two deputies led a shackled man into the sunlight. Ryder couldn't see much of him at first—just a lean figure in a dust-stained shirt, wrists bound in iron, stride steady as they walked him toward the noose. The crowd reacted instantly—some shouted curses, others spat into the dirt. Somewhere, a woman sobbed, the sound sharp and raw. The sheriff stepped up onto the platform, his voice steady as he read the charges.

"Murder."
"Horse theft."
"Robbery."
"Rape."

More shouts from the crowd. A man near the front looked like he was shaking with the effort not to lunge forward. Ryder didn't move. He just sipped his coffee, watching with dull patience. Then the prisoner turned toward the saloon.

And Ryder stopped cold.
He knew that face.

Ryder – Gone To Hell

The name Dale Madsen meant nothing to him. But the man standing on that gallows? That was Finn Crowe. Ryder knew him from years back, out in Arizona territory. Crowe had killed a Faro dealer over a bad hand, then shot up the saloon, killed three more before making his escape. Ryder had been part of the posse that had tried to track him down, but Crowe had slipped through their net.

Finn Crowe was the kind of man who didn't just kill to survive. He killed because he liked it. And now, he was staring straight at Ryder. A grin curled slowly over Crowe's face. Like he knew something Ryder didn't. A shiver ran down Ryder's spine, though he didn't let it show. Crowe deserved what was coming.

The sheriff gave the final words. "May God have mercy on your soul."

Ryder just kept watching. Because something didn't feel right.

The air in Wells Crossing felt thick with heat, dust, and vengeance.

The crowd had swelled, men and women pressing closer, the noose dangling like a snake waiting to strike. Faces were tight with fury or grief, some red with anger, others pale with something colder.

Ryder saw it all from his place near the saloon doors, sipping the last of his damn good coffee, watching the way folk had come together to see justice done. Some were here to watch a murderer die. Others, just to see if it would bring them peace.

A woman near the front wrung a handkerchief between her fingers, her shoulders shaking with quiet, broken sobs. Beside her, a man stood ramrod straight, his jaw clamped so tight Ryder half expected to hear his teeth crack. Off to the side, a rancher spat into the dust, shaking his head as he muttered something low under his breath. And then there were the kids—perched on wooden crates, hoisted onto their fathers' shoulders—wide-eyed and staring, their faces caught somewhere between fascination and fear. This was a story they'd tell for the rest of their lives. The day Dale Madsen swung.

Up on the gallows, Madsen stood with his wrists shackled in front of him, his head cocked just slightly as he took in the crowd. He looked bored, very much like a man watching a show he'd already seen too many times before. The preacher beside him cleared his throat, tugged at his collar, and lifted a well-worn Bible in one hand. His mouth was drawn into a firm line, his voice steady when he spoke.

"Dale Madsen," the preacher called loudly, his voice cutting through the uneasy silence. "You stand before the Lord and these good people. This is your last chance—

to seek forgiveness, to face your Maker with a clean heart, and accept His grace."

Madsen tilted his head, slow and deliberate. A smirk raised the corner of his mouth, and then, without a word, he leaned in and spat straight into the preacher's face. The square erupted. Shouts of outrage. Curses slung like stones. A woman's raw, broken sob split the air.

"Hang the bastard already!" a man near the front roared.

A deputy moved fast, striking Madsen hard across the face. The slap cracked through the morning stillness. Madsen's head snapped to the side, but when he turned back, blood at the corner of his mouth, he was grinning. Then he laughed. Low and quiet. A sound that crawled under the skin. Ryder felt it coil in his gut. The son of a bitch wasn't afraid, not one bit. He was enjoying this. The bastard wasn't scared.

The deputies yanked him forward, jerking him toward the noose. One of them pulled it tight over his head, cinching the knot with a rough tug. The sheriff stepped forward then, his voice even and unyielding.

"For your crimes against the people of this town," he said, "may God have mercy on your soul."

Madsen's grin widened. He shifted slightly, turning his head—just enough to find Ryder in the crowd. And he held his gaze. Not at the sheriff, not at the people who had lost family, who had waited to see him die, he stared at Ryder. That grin lingered. Ryder didn't move. Didn't blink. He just watched, his expression unreadable. The sheriff gave the signal. The trapdoor dropped and Madsen fell.

The rope snapped.

For a single breath, the world seemed to pause as Madsen hit the dirt below the platform with a dull, heavy thud. The crowd gasped as one. Some shouted in outrage, voices cracking with disbelief. A woman screamed. The deputies staggered back, frozen in place for a second, eyes wide. The preacher was pale as a ghost, his mouth slightly open, hands trembling, the bible he was holding dangling from his hands. Ryder's fingers tightened around his empty coffee cup.

Madsen groaned, then, to the horror of everyone watching, he pushed himself up onto his hands and knees, spitting dust and laughing. A sharp, wicked sound, full of something Ryder didn't like. The sheriff was already moving, hand going to his gun. Madsen lifted his head, that same damn grin still stretched across his face.

And Ryder, still standing in the doorway of the Silver Star, thought—

Well. Hell.

This wasn't over.

Ryder – Gone To Hell

Chapter 3 – The Shootout & Escape

For a moment, time held still.

The only sound was the creak of the broken rope swaying in the wind, the sharp, stunned silence of a crowd that had just watched a dead man fall and get back up.

Then—

Gunfire.

The first shot cracked from the back of the square, punching through the gallows post in a spray of splintered wood. The second found its mark. A deputy near the platform jerked suddenly as the bullet tore into his chest, the force of it sending him sprawling backward. His gun fell from his hand, clattering down the steps as the crowd erupted into screams.

More shots rang out, sharp and fast.

Madsen's men were here. They'd been hiding in the crowd, waiting for this moment—waiting for that rope to snap. Ryder moved before he thought, dropping his coffee cup and stepping back into the shadows of the Silver Star's doorway. He drew his gun in one smooth motion, his body moving with a kind of practiced calm that only came from years of living through worse.

Ryder – Gone To Hell

The square was chaos.

Men shoved past each other, trying to get clear. Women clutched at their children, pulling them toward cover. Through the chaos, Madsen was already moving. Lunging from under the platform. A horse waited at the edge of the square, held by a rider in a dust-worn duster, his rifle raised, covering Madsen's escape. Sheriff Rourke was on his feet, firing—but the shot went wide, ricocheting off the gallows steps as a bullet whined past his ear. One of Madsen's men stood near the water trough, rifle raised—lining up a shot at the sheriff.

Ryder saw it first.

Ryder leveled his Colt, his grip steady, the weight of the iron firm in his palm. The outlaw stood near the horse trough, a long rifle clutched in his hands, his coat dusty, face half-hidden beneath the low brim of a slouched hat. He wasn't some half-starved drifter—he had the build of a man who'd lived rough but eaten well, shoulders broad, his belt lined with bullets like a man expecting a long fight. The man wasn't looking Ryder's way. His focus was on the gallows, on Madsen, on the escape – on killing the sheriff.

His rifle lifted just slightly, lining up a shot. Ryder didn't let him take it. He fired once. The bullet punched a hole through cloth and then into the flesh beneath, lodging somewhere in the outlaw's ribs. His body jerked violently, feet stumbling, his ankles collapsing, and sending him backward, hat flying off as he toppled. He hit the horse trough hard, tipping the whole damn thing as he fell. The water exploded upward, splashing in a wide arc as his body half-submerged, arms flailing. For a moment, Ryder caught a look at his face—a bearded man with mean, sun-creased features, mouth open in a final, choking gasp before his head slipped under the water. His rifle clattered from his fingers, falling to the street. The water around him darkened, rippling with something red.

Ryder didn't wait to see if he got up. He was already moving.

One of Madsen's men grabbed the saddle horn, holding the horse steady as the outlaw arrived. More gunfire ripped through the square, but Madsen didn't pay any attention to it. He threw himself up onto the saddle, his heels already in the horse's sides before he had a tight grip on the reins, already spurring the horse forward. A deputy fired wildly, the shot missing by a mile. Sheriff Rourke raised his gun again, but before he could pull the trigger, another shot from the crowd sent him diving for cover.

The Shot That Never Landed

Ryder – Gone To Hell

Ryder tracked Madsen's movement; his body relaxed, breathing even, the Colt, an extension of his hand.

The outlaw was nothing but a shape in the dust, a moving target between the gallows and the edge of town. Ryder had made shots harder than this before.

His grip tightened, the sights lining up cleanly.

His finger tensed on the trigger.

Then—

A blur of movement.

A woman rushed into his line of fire, shawl flying behind her like a broken-winged bird. She didn't see him. Didn't even know he was there. Her arms were outstretched, reaching—toward someone in the crowd or maybe just toward something already lost. Tears tracked down her dust-streaked face, her voice lost beneath the gunfire and shouting.

Damn it.

Ryder cursed, twisting his wrist at the last second, instincts taking over. The shot snapped wide, the bullet whining upward, splintering the wooden overhang of the general store. A sharp crack rang out as bits of shattered timber rained onto the boardwalk. The woman didn't even flinch—she kept running, her shawl dragging through the dust behind her.

Wyatt Steele

Ryder let out a slow breath through his nose, lowering his gun. He'd nearly shot her. Damn near took her head off. And now Madsen was gone, out of range.

Madsen spurred his horse hard, and horse and rider tore from the square, a laugh spilling from his mouth as if this whole thing had been nothing but a huge joke. His men were already riding after him, kicking up a dust cloud as they bolted for the open desert, leaving the gasping and shocked townsfolk behind. A last wild shot cracked from the rooftops, but it was far too late. The outlaws disappeared into the hills, their dust trail fading into the wind. Ryder let out a slow, even breath, slipping his Colt back into the holster.

Texas Bill appeared at Ryder's side, a shotgun clasped tight in his hands, but there was nothing left to shoot at. He let out a low whistle, shaking his head. "Damn shame, cowboy. Would've been one hell of a shot."

Ryder didn't answer. Instead, he turned his eyes back to the gallows—to the frayed, swaying rope. Someone had cut it. Madsen's gang had been waiting for this. This wasn't luck. It was a plan. And now, Wells Crossing wasn't just missing a dead man. It had a bigger problem.

The dust still hung thick in the air, turning the morning sunlight into a hazy yellow. Gunpowder clung to the wind, mixing with the sweat of frightened people, the sharp iron scent of blood, and the crushed dirt kicked up by Madsen's escape.

Chaos reigned.

Men shouted, cursing the law, cursing the outlaws, cursing the whole damn mess. Women wept, clutching their children, faces buried in handkerchiefs, trembling hands smoothing down skirts that had no need of it. A stray horse, wild-eyed and riderless, bolted down the street, its reins trailing in the dirt; it probably belonged to the outlaw Ryder had shot. The kids had noticed the dead man as well. A small pack of curious boys had already edged toward the horse trough, eyes wide with morbid fascination.

Ryder barely spared them a glance. Instead, he and Texas Bill walked toward the gallows, stepping over spent shells, past men with angry, red faces, and past the ones who just stood in stunned silence. Texas let out a low whistle. The broken noose still hung from the gallows beam, swaying in the wind like a bad omen. The cut was clean. Right where the rope looped over the wood, where no one would have noticed it.

Texas pointed at the frayed edges of the hemp. "Son of a bitch," he muttered. "Wasn't no accident."

Ryder didn't respond. He was pretty sure that was obvious: the outlaw's gang among the spectators and the getaway horse standing by. Yeah, it was definitely not an accident. Someone had climbed up here in the dead of night and sawed through that rope, knowing damn well what would happen. Someone had planned the whole damned escape.

The deputy who had been shot had rolled down the steps, and the town doctor knelt beside him, pressing a bloodied cloth to the man's chest. The deputy's breathing was shallow, his skin gray beneath the morning light. His wife sat beside him, clutching his hand in both of hers, her shoulders shaking as she sobbed.

"You're gonna be fine, James," she whispered, rocking slightly as if saying it enough times would make it true.

The doctor's face told another story. His jaw was tight, his expression grave. "This is bad," the doc was muttering under his breath.

The sheriff stood nearby, his hand white-knuckled on his holster, watching the doc work. Ryder didn't envy him. One of his men was dying, and his town had just been humiliated. The law had been made a fool of today.

Sheriff Joss Rourke turned suddenly, his voice rising like the crack of a rifle shot. "Enough!" The word ripped through the square, cutting through the muttering, the cursing, the nervous whispers. The raw anger in his voice stilled the crowd and made folks blink and shift uneasily in their boots. "Get back to your business! This town ain't lawless!"

The people hesitated. Because for the last ten minutes, it sure as hell had been. The law had been humiliated in front of its own people. A man had been sentenced to die, and instead, he'd ridden off laughing, leaving a body in his wake. The town had watched, helpless, terrified. And that kind of thing? It stuck. Rourke knew it. His jaw clenched, his eyes flashing as he scanned the square, daring anyone to challenge him.

A few men grumbled low, pulling their hats down as they turned away, slipping back into the rhythm of their day. Work still needed doing, and most weren't looking for trouble.

But some lingered. Their eyes stayed locked on the gallows, on the dark stain soaking into the dirt where the deputy had fallen.

Ryder could see it in their faces

The hesitation.

The fear.

Rourke wasn't about to let that take root. He turned on his heel, facing what was left of his deputies—the few who hadn't hit the dirt today.

"Madsen won't make it far." His voice cut through the silence, solid and sure. "We'll run him down before sundown."

Wyatt Steele

The words hung in the air, a challenge as much as a promise.

He swept a look across the gathered men, gauging them, testing them.

"I'm riding after him. Any man willing to help can meet me at the jailhouse in an hour."

Then he waited, his steely gaze daring someone to step up—or to walk away.

A low murmur rippled through the square, the kind of restless movement that came when a crowd started thinking twice. Some men stiffened, rolling their shoulders back, hands shifting toward their belts, casting sideways glances at one another.

But the rest?

They hesitated.

This wasn't their fight. That was for the law to handle.

Near the front, a rancher shifted uncomfortably, muttering something about checking his stock. A storekeeper's wife grabbed hold of her husband's sleeve, whispering urgently in his ear.

A carpenter rubbed his palms against his trousers, shaking his head as he slipped quietly toward the safety of his shop.

On I'll one, the crowd that had been so eager for blood just moments ago" started to thin.

But not all of them.

Ryder – Gone To Hell

A handful remained. Men with hard eyes and steady hands. The kind that didn't back down.

Rourke's gaze locked onto Ryder. No words were spoken, but the message was clear enough. Ryder wasn't one of them. Didn't belong to this town or its problems. But today, he'd drawn his iron.

And that meant he was in it now.

Texas tilted his head, a slow smirk tugging at the corner of his mouth. "What's your move, cowboy?"

Ryder exhaled through his nose, his eyes sliding back toward the gallows. The noose still swayed gently, the wind mocking the empty space where a man should be hanging. Madsen had dodged his fate. For now. But Ryder had seen men slip the rope before. And most of them didn't get lucky twice. The only question was who was gonna send him the rest of the way.

Ryder adjusted his hat, tilting it low over his eyes. "Well," he muttered, voice dry, "suppose I got an hour to kill."

Wyatt Steele

Ryder – Gone To Hell
Chapter 4 – The Posse Rides

Ryder stepped through the swinging doors of the Silver Star, the scent of fresh coffee and frying bacon meeting him like a warm handshake. The saloon was quieter now—most of the town still lingering outside, talking about the mess left behind in the square. But the tension still hung thick in the air, the kind that didn't settle easy. He barely made it two steps before Lila Jay spotted him.

She wiped her hands on her apron, strode over, and caught his arm with surprising force, steering him toward a table near the bar. "You sit there, cowboy, and don't move."

Ryder didn't argue. Lila Jay wasn't the kind of woman you argued with. She disappeared into the kitchen, and two minutes later, she was back, setting down a fresh plate in front of him—eggs, bacon, thick slices of buttered cornbread. A fresh cup of coffee followed immediately after. Ryder glanced at her, one brow raised.

She just smirked, crossing her arms over her chest. "You look like the kind of fella who could manage a second helping."

Wyatt Steele

Ryder glanced down at the plate. Didn't disagree.

"Besides," she added, "it's my pleasure."

"Much appreciated, ma'am." Ryder tipped his hat slightly, then picked up his fork. Good cooking was good cooking. And the coffee? Damn, it was good.

Outside, the town hadn't quite settled. The gallows still stood broken, the blood on the ground not yet dry, and folks were still talking in tight clusters about Madsen's escape. Some were watching the jailhouse, where men were gathering for the posse. And a handful of curious boys had another idea entirely.

From under the saloon's batwing doors, a row of small, dirt-streaked faces peeked in, wide-eyed and whispering in excited tones. They weren't looking for Texas Bill. They were looking at Ryder. The man who'd drawn on an outlaw and shot him dead.

Texas Bill, standing near the bar, caught sight of them and let out a low chuckle. "Damn kids," he muttered. Then he took one big step forward, clapping his hands together loudly. "Git!"

The boys let out a chorus of yelps, scattering like chickens before a coyote. One tripped over his own feet, and another lost his hat in the dirt. They kicked up dust as they ran, laughing and shouting.

Ryder – Gone To Hell

Texas grinned, shaking his head. "Ain't got no damn sense."

Ryder sipped his coffee. Didn't smile, but didn't not smile either. He took another bite of bacon and let the moment settle. It was probably the last quiet one he'd have today.

The sun had climbed in the sky, baking the dust into the hard-packed road as Ryder and Texas Bill strode toward the sheriff's office. The town was still buzzing with tension, folk talking in tight whispers outside storefronts, others gathered in the saloon, nursing drinks and muttering about the outlaw who should have swung. They wanted justice. But most weren't willing to chase it down. That was up to the men waiting outside Sheriff Rourke's office.

There were six of them in total. Sheriff Joss Rourke stood on the porch, arms folded, watching as the last of the volunteers arrived. Texas strode up with easy confidence, his shotgun still balanced over one shoulder. Ryder followed boots scuffing against the boardwalk. The others were already waiting. Rourke gave them all a long look, nodding at each one.

"Tom. Damned sorry about your brother. He was a fine deputy, a loss to the town," he said, acknowledging Calder first. A short nod in return, a lean, hard-eyed man, his face tight with grief and anger. His

Wyatt Steele

brother had died ten minutes ago, but he wasn't crying. He was here to kill a man.

"Will, good to see you," Rourke said to Will Tanner, a ranch hand with strong shoulders and quiet eyes; he looked to Ryder like the kind of man who spoke little but listened well. Tanner just nodded by way of reply.

"Harlan, sure can use your help," Rourke said to a man wearing an army coat. Ryder would later find out he was a former cavalry scout turned farrier who looked like he'd rather be shoeing horses than chasing down killers—but he was here anyway.

Last, there was the kid.

"Ethan, you sure about this? Your Pa know?" the Sherrif said to the kid. Ethan Doyle, young, maybe nineteen or twenty, a rail-thin cowboy with something to prove. He looked determined but too eager—the kind of man who got himself killed if he wasn't careful. Ethan's cheeks flushed in embarrassment. "Yeah, he knows."

"Texas, glad to see you," Rourke said, "Can always use a man handy with a shotgun."

Texas nodded and gave a grim smile in return.

Rourke then turned to the last man, his remaining deputy, Sam Upton. He'd lost a friend today, and it showed in his tight jaw and steely expression. "Sam's my second in command. You remember that."

Ryder – Gone To Hell

Rourke's eyes landed on Ryder. Assessing. Measuring. "And you?"

Ryder glanced at Texas. Texas just smirked, saying nothing. Rourke didn't press, just waited. After a beat, Ryder shrugged. "Name's Ryder."

The sheriff narrowed his eyes slightly. "You ever hunted a man before?"

Ryder adjusted his hat. "Seen Madsen before. Down in Arizona, near Tucson. Went by the name of Finn Crowe."

That got a reaction. The name wasn't unfamiliar to a few of the men standing there. Rourke's gaze sharpened. "Crowe?"

Ryder gave a slow nod. "Shot up a saloon, killed a Faro dealer. Killed a few more before he made his escape."

Rourke exhaled sharply, shaking his head. "Well, ain't that somethin'." For a moment, he just studied Ryder. Then his eyes narrowed slightly, his gaze settling on Ryder's features. "You're a bounty hunter." It wasn't an insult, just a statement of fact.

Ryder didn't react. He just nodded once. "Have been, worked for the law, worn a badge and taken my turn at running herds as well."

Rourke nodded. "Good." Then he turned to the rest of them. "You men understand what we're doing here?" His voice was gruff, steady. "This ain't a bounty hunt. This ain't some glory ride. Madsen killed a deputy today. He killed folks before that. We're bringing him to justice."

He let the weight of that settle. A few nods.

Tom Calder gritted his teeth. "Justice, yeah."

Rourke held his gaze for a second longer, then nodded. "Raise your right hand."

They did.

"For the duration of this hunt, you are deputies of Wells Crossing. Your duty is to uphold the law, bring Dale Madsen to justice, and ride in the service of this town. You will not dishonor the badge. You will not act as outlaws. If a man draws against you, you may defend yourself. But we take Madsen alive, if possible. Swear it."

Each man gave his oath, some quiet, some louder.

Texas glanced at Ryder and smirked. "Damn, cowboy," he muttered, "guess that makes you official."

Ryder didn't say anything. He just lowered his hand and adjusted his hat.

Rourke buckled his gun belt tighter. "We ride in an hour."

The men scattered to gather their gear, to get their horses, to say whatever last words needed saying. Ryder just watched the dust swirl in the morning light. Madsen had cheated the noose. But he wasn't going to cheat the bullet.

Ryder – Gone To Hell

Ryder climbed the stairs of the Silver Star slowly, his boots sounding heavier than usual against the well-worn wood. Inside his room, the air was still and quiet, the scent of soap and fresh linens hanging in the warmth. For a second, he just stood there, taking in the kind of comfort he'd hardly had time to enjoy. The kind he didn't get often. The kind he knew he wouldn't get again anytime soon. With a slow sigh, he reached for his saddlebags, packing up what little he had. Ryder slung his bags over his shoulder, took one last glance around the quiet space, and headed downstairs.

He barely made it two steps into the saloon before Lila Jay was in front of him, blocking his path. She had something wrapped in a cloth, still warm from the stove, and before he could even protest, she shoved it into his hands.

"For the road," she said simply.

Ryder hesitated, a little embarrassed.

She lifted a brow. "Don't you dare try to give it back."

He didn't. Instead, he nodded, shifting the bundle in his grip.

Lila Jay smirked, crossing her arms. "You bring yourself back here, cowboy. And when you do, I'll cook you a steak like you've never had before."

Wyatt Steele

Ryder adjusted his hat, shifting the warm bundle in his hands. "Thanks, ma'am," he said, voice low, a little rough around the edges. He wasn't much for words, and gratitude always sat awkwardly on his tongue. Still, Lila Jay just grinned, like she saw right through him. Ryder gave a small nod, then stepped out onto the boardwalk, tucking the bundle into his saddlebag.

The morning sun was higher now, stretching shadows long across the street. At the livery, Willy Scott already had Sparks saddled and ready, the buckskin mare stamping her hooves against the dirt.

"Figured you'd need her ready," Willy said, tightening the girth one last time.

Ryder reached into his coat, pulling out a couple of coins for the night's livery.

Willy waved him off, shaking his head. "You can pay when you come back."

Ryder hesitated, then tucked the coins away. He didn't argue. He just mounted up, settling into the saddle like it was where he belonged. He rode out of the livery, turning toward the sheriff's office, where the posse was waiting.

The sun sat high and hot as the posse gathered in the street, the last of the supplies loaded, rifles checked, and canteens slung over saddles. Sheriff Rourke took the lead, and his deputy Sam Upton was at his side. The others—Texas Bill, Tom

Ryder – Gone To Hell

Calder, Will Tanner, Ethan Doyle, and Harlan Pritchard—fell in behind them, their horses shifting restlessly beneath them, sensing the weight in the air. Ryder rode with them. But he didn't feel like he did. He was part of this group but separate from it—a man riding alongside them, not with them. That was the way it always was.

The town hadn't come out in force, but a handful of folks stood on porches along the boardwalks, watching them go. A shopkeeper leaned against his doorway, arms folded, eyes full of something unreadable. A few women clutched handkerchiefs, nodding solemnly.

And then there were the shouts.

"Go get the damn bastard!"

"Bring him back in irons!"

"Stay safe out there!"

"Don't let him slip you!"

Some of it was anger. Some was hope. Most of it was just fear masked in different ways. Ryder just kept riding.

As they neared the edge of town, the undertaker's cart was there. The dead outlaw from earlier lay sprawled in the back, arms hanging limp, boots sticking out from beneath a rough sheet. A few boys loitered nearby, gaping at the corpse, their faces full of a mix of excitement and horror. One of them kicked at the dust, murmuring something to another before they all scattered as the posse rode past.

    Ryder barely spared them a glance.

    Rourke lifted his reins. "Let's ride."

    The posse left Wells Crossing behind, dust kicking up in their wake. The town grew smaller behind them, the desert stretching ahead.

Chapter 5 – A Bad Trail to Follow

The sun WAS low in the sky, burning red against the horizon as the posse picked its way across the open plains, heading toward the rugged hills ahead. Ryder rode near the front alongside Rourke, his eyes scanning the ground for signs. The dust, the hoof marks, the disturbed sagebrush—all of it told a story. Madsen was heading for the canyons. He knew these men were chasing him. He knew they'd come fast. And he also knew he'd have the advantage if he could get them into the rocks by nightfall.

Sheriff Rourke reined up beside him. "How's the trail?"

Ryder nodded ahead. "He's running for the hills. No doubt about it."

Rourke looked ahead at the darkening sky, his jaw tightening. "Think we can catch him before he gets there?"

Ryder shook his head. "Not unless you want to ride straight into an ambush."

That made Rourke frown.

"If we push on now, we'll be too close to the rocks by nightfall," Ryder continued. "Madsen could be hiding in those canyons.

Wyatt Steele

We won't have cover. Best stop for the night. Pick up the trail at first light."

The sheriff mulled it over, glancing at his men. None of them were green, but chasing an outlaw into dark country wasn't a smart move. He gave a sharp nod. "We camp here."

The order was given, and the men began dismounting, tying up their horses, and setting up a small fire. The land was flat, open enough that they'd have a good view of anything coming at them in the night. But Ryder knew Madsen wouldn't come at them. Not yet. He was too smart for that.

The fire crackled low, throwing flickering shadows across the ground as the posse settled in, passing around rations and rolling cigarettes. Tom Calder sat a little apart from the others, staring into the flames, his hands clenched around a tin cup. His brother had died not ten minutes before he'd taken the oath to chase Madsen down, and the weight of it had settled deep in his bones. Ryder had seen that kind of grief before. The kind that burned hot. Too hot. He'd seen what revenge could do to a man. It made you careless. Made you blind to the trap ahead.

Rourke sat near Tom, saying nothing, just letting the man sit with his thoughts.

Across the fire, Texas Bill pulled a bottle from his saddlebag. "Figured we might need this," he said with a grin, holding up

Ryder – Gone To Hell

the whiskey bottle he'd grabbed from the saloon.

The tension eased just a fraction as he uncorked it and took the first swig, then passed it around. Sam Upton took a drink, then Rourke. Tom hesitated, then took the bottle and tipped it back. Ryder didn't reach for it. He just listened.

The talk turned to Madsen, to the kind of men who thought they could run from justice. Then Rourke turned to Ryder. "Tell us what happened in the saloon, Ryder. Back when Madsen was calling himself Finn Crowe."

Ryder didn't say anything at first. He never liked telling stories. But they were all looking at him now, so he finally sighed and leaned back against his saddle. The fire crackled and popped, sending embers swirling into the night air. The men sat quiet, listening, their faces flickering with the light, eyes locked on Ryder as he spoke. He didn't rush the telling. Didn't embellish. Just laid it down straight.

"It was a place outside Tucson," he said, staring into the flames. "One of those saloons that had seen better days but wasn't done yet. It was big enough for regular games, with a few good rooms upstairs, but small enough that folks kept their business quiet. I was there that night. Not at the Faro table, but close enough to see the play.

Wyatt Steele

Crowe came in like any other man. Sat down, laid his money on the felt, and played slow, steady. Losing just enough to make it look like he was down on his luck. The dealer was a man named Jonah Hayes. Run the table like he'd been born behind it. Fair player. Knew how to handle himself. Crowe played for nearly an hour, kept his bets small, and never said much. Jonah barely looked at him—figured he was just another cowpoke about to lose his wages and walk out with empty pockets. Only, that wasn't how it went."

Ryder paused and took a slow breath. The firelight danced in his calm, unreadable gaze.

Ethan Doyle leaned forward, hanging on every word. "Then what happened?"

Ryder didn't look at him. "Then Crowe flipped the table and shot Jonah in the gut."

The fire popped loudly. The men around the fire barely breathed.

Ryder went on, his voice steady. "Wasn't any shouting, no argument. No warning. One second, he was losing his hand; the next, Jonah was choking on his own blood. Then Crowe turned his gun left and right shot two more before the room even realized what was happening.

Ethan blinked. "Just like that?"

Ryder nodded. "Just like that. There was a man named Elias Greeley in the corner that night; an ex-lawman still carried a badge when it suited him. He was quicker than most. Drew on Crowe, got a shot off. But Crowe was faster. Shot him clean through the chest."

Someone let out a slow breath, shifting their seat.

"By then, the saloon had turned into a damn slaughterhouse. Women screaming, men diving for cover, a bottle of whiskey shattered on the floor and mixed with the blood. By the time I got my gun drawn, Crowe was already moving. He backed toward the doors, gun in each hand, watching every face. Looking for someone stupid enough to try and stop him. I wasn't stupid. But I wasn't about to let him ride out easy, either. When he hit the street, I was the first out the door after him." Ryder let the words hang there a moment. "Got a shot off. Missed. He fired back didn't. Took a chunk outta the doorframe right where my head had been a second before. He went for his horse."

Ethan's brow furrowed. "So you rode after him?"

Ryder nodded.

"Not just me. Sheriff out of Tucson got a posse together before the hour was out. We rode hard, maybe six, seven men. Good trackers. Good shots. But Crowe was slippery. He Rode fast and ditched his trail when he could. Kept moving through the valleys, cutting through canyons. Figured we had him when we found his camp a few days out. But he was already gone. The last tracks led south. Straight for the border."

Texas Bill let out a breath. "So the bastard got away."

Ryder gave a slow nod. "We figured he made it into Mexico. Didn't have the authority to chase him past the line. So that was it. The trail went cold. Finn Crowe was gone."

The fire crackled again, sending sparks into the night. The posse sat silent for a moment, the weight of the story settling on them.

Ethan shook his head. "And now he's Madsen."

Ryder looked up, meeting the kid's eyes. "No," he said evenly. "He's the same man he always was."

The words settled deep. There was a long pause, the firelight flickering against hard, thoughtful faces.

Then Nathan Briggs, the former army scout, snorted and shifted. "Sounds like a hell of a story." Something in his voice had a sharp edge to it.

Ryder flicked his eyes toward him. Nathan's face was tight, his jaw working.

"Something wrong with it?" Ryder asked, voice easy.

Nathan rolled his shoulders, letting out a slow breath. Then, looking across the fire at Rourke, he said, "Just seems like you put a lot of faith in someone you just met over someone you actually know, Sheriff."

The fire went still. Texas Bill's grin faded instantly. Tom Calder lifted his head from his drink. For a long second, no one spoke. Rourke didn't jump to reply. He just stared at Nathan; the flames reflected in his sharp eyes.

Then he reached for the bottle, took a sip, and passed it straight to Nathan. "You got a problem with the way I run my posse, Nathan?"

Nathan hesitated.

He looked at the bottle. Then at Ryder.

Then he shook his head. "No, sir."

He took the whiskey and drank. But Ryder could tell. It wasn't over.

Across from him, Will Tanner—the ranch hand—reached out, clapping Nathan on the arm. "I hear you." His voice was low, friendly. "Ain't much sense trusting a man you don't know."

Nathan didn't say anything. But he nodded.

And Ryder just watched.

The morning came slow and gray, mist clinging to the low brush, softening the edges of the land as the posse stirred from their makeshift camp. The embers of last night's fire still smoldered, sending up thin, curling tendrils of smoke into the dawn air. Ryder sat on his haunches, staring at the cup of coffee in his hands. It was strong, bitter, and burnt, but it was hot, and that was about all a man could ask for in the wild. He took a sip, letting the heat wake him up, even if the taste did nothing for him. It wasn't Lila Jay's coffee. Not even close.

 Texas Bill muttered a curse as he poured himself a cup, shaking his head. "Damn thing could peel the paint off a barn."

 Ryder took another sip. "Still coffee."

 Texas huffed but didn't argue. They all needed it. Tom Calder sat near the fire, staring into the flames, silent, his cup untouched. Ethan Doyle sat a little ways off, fiddling with the buckle on his gun belt, trying to hide the nervous energy sitting under his skin. Nathan Briggs stood off to the side, rolling his shoulders and adjusting his saddle, his mood still sour from the night before. And Will Tanner? He just watched. He didn't say much.

 They saddled up as the mist began to lift, revealing the rolling terrain ahead, the hills waiting for them in the distance. Ryder took his time, adjusting Sparks's cinch and checking the bridle. He wasn't in any hurry to lead. That was Nathan's job today. If the man wanted to prove himself, Ryder was more than happy to let him. He mounted up, reining Sparks around, and fell to the back of the group, keeping his eyes on the trail, the riders, and everything in between.

Nathan took the lead, rolling his shoulders before nudging his horse forward, his gaze fixed ahead like he was determined to prove something. Maybe to Rourke. Maybe to himself. Maybe just to Ryder. Didn't much matter.

The posse moved out, leaving their campfire smoldering in the dirt, the morning wind carrying the last of the heat away. The chase was back on. They found signs of a camp not long after. Nathan reined up, scanning the ground. The posse pulled in behind him, forming a loose circle as eyes swept over the scene. The fire had burned low, just blackened coals in the dirt, the ground stamped down by horses and boots. A few whiskey bottles lay discarded nearby, some shattered, some rolling loose in the dust.

Madsen had been here. Not long ago.

Ryder swung a leg over and dismounted, crouching near the fire pit. He pressed a hand against the ashes.

Warm.

Not much, but enough to tell him they weren't far behind.

Texas Bill nudged a whiskey bottle with the toe of his boot. "Left in a hurry."

Wyatt Steele

Rourke sighed through his nose, scanning the hills beyond. "They knew we'd be coming."

Tom Calder dismounted, hands on his hips, scowling hard. "Then we need to move."

Ethan squinted down at the ground. "Which way'd they go?"

All eyes turned to Nathan. Nathan straightened, adjusting his belt, then pointed toward the rising hills. "They're running for the canyons."

Ryder said nothing. But he already knew what lay ahead. The signs were clear. The posse wasn't just hunting. They were being led. And somewhere out there, in the rocks and the brush, A trap was waiting.

Ryder – Gone To Hell
Chapter 6 – An Ambush in the Rocks

The land began to shift, the flat sprawl of the plains giving way to rougher country, where the earth rose in jagged formations, hard and cracked from years beneath the sun. The wind had changed too—no longer rolling easily across open ground but funneled tight through rocky outcroppings, carrying dust and heat with it.

The hills ahead were like the spine of something ancient, the canyons between them deep and winding, the kind of place where a few good men with steady rifles could turn a pursuit into a slaughter. Ryder rode near the rear of the posse, letting his eyes drift over the land, reading the story it told.

The trail was too clean. Too easy. Madsen wasn't just running. He was leading them. Nathan Briggs rode ahead, his back straight as a steel bar, shoulders squared like a man with something to prove. He was riding too fast, too sure of himself, too confident about the way the trail wound through the hills.

That made Ryder uneasy.

Didn't like how the trail seemed to be leading them exactly where Madsen would want them. Didn't like that Rourke wasn't questioning it. Didn't like that no one else was either. Finally, Ryder clicked his tongue and nudged Sparks forward, drawing up beside the sheriff.

Rourke glanced at him. "Something wrong?"

"We should circle wide," Ryder said, voice low and steady.

Rourke's eyes narrowed slightly. "You saying we should turn tail?"

"I'm saying I've followed this bastard before." Ryder kept his voice even, but there was weight in it, something solid. "Madsen's smart. He's fast. And if I was him, I'd be holed up in these rocks, waiting for us to walk into a damn trap."

Ahead, Nathan let out a sharp bark of laughter. "Ain't that something?" He half-turned in the saddle, smirking, his face catching the last burn of the sun. "The great Ryder, the gunfighter, worried about a little canyon. Thought you had ice in your veins."

A few of the others shifted in their saddles, glancing between Nathan and Ryder. Tom Calder kept his eyes forward, his face hard and unreadable. Ethan Doyle looked uneasy, his grip tightening on the reins. Texas Bill let out a long breath through his nose, watching but saying nothing. Ryder didn't bite. Didn't rise to it. Didn't blink.

Instead, he just looked at Nathan, his face empty, his voice quiet but sure. "You've never seen what he's capable of, have you?"

Nathan's smirk didn't fade, but there was something else behind it now, something thin and stretched. "I know cowards when I see 'em."

The words hung sharp in the air, cutting through the stillness. Rourke didn't say anything. Nobody did.

The canyon loomed ahead, its entrance yawning wide like a mouth waiting to swallow them whole. Texas Bill let out a breath through his nose, watching from a little ways back, but didn't say anything. Neither did Ryder. He just looked back at Rourke.

The sheriff hesitated. Then he exhaled and shook his head. "We ride through. No turning back now."

Ryder didn't argue. But he kept his hand near his gun.

The ground turned rough beneath the horses' hooves, hard-packed dirt giving way to uneven rock, the kind that forced a rider to slow or risk a broken leg on his mount. The posse eased back, the rhythm of hooves shifting from a steady thump-thump-thump to a more cautious, deliberate pace. Ryder let his gaze drift upward toward the rising canyon walls ahead, his eyes sweeping every ledge, every jagged outcrop. The shadows were growing longer, stretching deep into the narrow spaces between the rocks.

He didn't like this.

Didn't like how the wind had died down, how the brush was still, how even the usual distant call of a hawk had gone silent.

No birds.

No movement.

Just the faint sound of leather creaking, hooves scuffing against the rocky ground, and the occasional snort from a horse. His gut pulled tight. He flicked a glance at Texas Bill, who was riding just behind him. Texas must've felt it, too, because he gave a small shake of his head, mouth set in a hard line.

Something wasn't right.

Ahead, Nathan Briggs led the way, still riding too damn sure of himself, his eyes locked straight ahead as they approached the break in the rock wall. The entrance to the canyon. It loomed wide before them, a natural cut in the stone, just wide enough for them to ride two abreast. The kind of place a man would pick to make a stand. Ryder tightened his grip on the reins, his thumb resting near the hammer of his Colt. The canyon swallowed them up, one by one, its walls rising high on either side, the sunlight casting long, jagged shadows against the stone. The air was thicker here, heavier, the walls of the canyon pressing in like the ribs of a dying beast, trapping heat, holding silence.

Ryder felt it before it happened.

That old, familiar pull in his gut, the one that told a man when the air was about to turn black with gunpowder when the next breath might be his last. His fingers hovered near his Colt, his eyes moving over the ledges above, searching the jagged shadows, waiting for the first movement—

Then—

A sharp crack split the air, loud as thunder.

The first shot hit just inches from Rourke's head, exploding into the canyon wall, sending shards of rock spitting into the air like shattered glass. The second came fast, kicking up a spray of dust just in front of Ryder's horse.

For half a heartbeat, everything held still.

Then—

Chaos.

"Take cover!" Rourke barely got the words out before the posse scattered.

Another shot rang out, this one slamming into the shoulder of a nearby rock, sending fragments whining past Ryder's ear. He dropped from the saddle without thinking, boots hitting hard dirt and rolling fast behind a boulder. Gunfire poured down from the ledges above.

Wyatt Steele

Madsen's men had been waiting for them. The narrow canyon walls turned the gunfire into an echoing storm, the reports bouncing off the stone in a deafening, endless roar. Ryder took a breath, slow and steady, his heart beating like a drum against his ribs. He stole a glance around what cover there was.

Movement.

Dark shapes against the rock, silhouettes crouching, rifles glinting in the sunlight—Then, the flash of a muzzle.

A bullet whined past his cheek, close enough that he felt the heat of it as it tore through the air. He didn't hesitate. He lined up a shot aimed at the man who had just fired on him. A tattered brown coat. A rifle shouldered for another shot—Ryder squeezed the trigger. The outlaw jerked backward as the bullet hit, his body snapping against the canyon wall before crumpling into a lifeless heap.

Another shadow moved up high, a second man fumbling to reload, his hands shaky. A shot cracked—this one from Rourke—the second man went down before he could chamber the next round. Still, the shooting didn't stop. Ethan Doyle was firing wild, his shots too high, too fast, bullets kicking up dust, shattering stone but hitting nothing. Nathan was moving low, pressing toward the left, barking orders like he'd been waiting for this.

Ryder – Gone To Hell

Will Tanner had his rifle up, crouched behind a boulder. Will wasn't firing. Just watching, maybe trying to line up a shot. The fight stretched on, the canyon ringing with gunfire, dust, and smoke thick in the air.

Then, as quickly as it had begun—

It was over. The last of the echoes rolled out into the distance, fading. Silence settled in. Madsen's men were gone and vanished back into the rocks. For a second, no one moved. The air was thick with gunpowder and sweat, the smell of blood settling into the dirt.

Then a voice rang out, sharp and raw. "Sam's down!"

Ryder turned. Sam Upton—the sheriff's deputy, a man who had sworn an oath to uphold the law—was crumpled in the dirt. Ryder could tell he was dead before he reached him. The right side of his head was gone, torn open by a close shot. A clean, brutal wound. Rourke stood over him, jaw clenched tight, eyes hard. Tom Calder let out a slow breath, his hands shaking as he ran a palm over his mouth. Ethan Doyle just stared, his face pale.

Texas Bill sighed, tipping his hat back. "Damn shame."

Ryder wasn't looking at the body anymore. He was looking at the canyon walls. Something wasn't right. The shots from the ambush had all come from above, from Madsen's men in the rocks. But Sam's wound? That shot had come from closer in. Much closer. And only three men had been near enough to pull the trigger. Ethan. Will. Nathan.

Ryder said nothing. He just let his eyes move over them, one by one. And for the first time since this chase started—He felt something worse than doubt.

The desert was cruel ground for a grave. Dry and unforgiving, it held nothing, kept nothing, offered nothing. It swallowed men whole, bleached their bones under the sun, and let the wind carry the rest away. There was no choice in it. They couldn't take Sam Upton with them. Couldn't lay him across a horse and haul him through the hills like some broken sack of meat while they rode after Madsen. So, they'd bury him where he fell. No time for digging. Just rocks. The men worked in tired, bitter silence, hauling stones from the canyon floor and piling them over what was left of their dead companion. It took time, too much time.

With every second spent moving rocks, Madsen got farther away. Tom Calder worked fast and hard, like a man who wanted the job done so he could stop thinking. His jaw was tight, his eyes dark and distant. Ethan Doyle moved slower, his face pale, his hands shaking as he dropped each stone onto the growing mound. Texas Bill stacked the rocks without a word, his usual smirk nowhere to be found. Nathan and Will were side by side, working steadily. Ryder lifted a rock and set it into place, then another, and another. One more weight on the pile.

Pointless, in the end. Coyotes would find their way in. Buzzards would finish what they left. That was just the way of the desert. But they did it anyway. When it was done, they stood around the rough pile of stones, heads lowered, sweat drying on their faces.

Sheriff Rourke cleared his throat, brushing dust from his hands. He looked at the grave, then at his men. His voice was gruff and steady, but the weight behind it was real. "Sam Upton was a good man. He stood for the law, and he died fighting for it. Ain't much else a man can do in this life."

A pause.

Then—quieter, rougher—"Rest easy, Sam."

No one spoke after that. There wasn't much left to say. One by one, they turned back toward their horses, dusting their hands and adjusting their belts. Madsen was running. And now, he had a few hours on them.

Nathan Briggs kept stealing glances at Ryder. Small, quick looks. Watching him.

Measuring him. Ryder noticed but didn't react. Didn't acknowledge it. He just adjusted his hat and swung into the saddle. Nathan didn't stop looking. The tension in him built like storm clouds, gathering, darkening, ready to break. Finally, he snapped.

"Go on, say it!" Nathan's words came sharp and fast, cutting through the quiet like a gunshot. Every head turned. Nathan's face was red and angry, and his hands curled into fists around his reins. "You want to blame me for this, don't you?"

Ryder didn't answer. Didn't rise to it. Just watched him, his expression unreadable.

Nathan's breath came sharp and ragged. "You think I led us into this? You think I got Sam killed?" The fire was hot in his voice.

Ryder sighed through his nose. He wasn't in the mood for this.

Rourke's voice cut in, calm but firm. "That's enough, Nathan."

Nathan let out a breath, shaking his head.

Will Tanner reached out and clapped a hand on Nathan's shoulder. "Ain't worth it."

Ryder – Gone To Hell

Nathan didn't look convinced. But he held his tongue.

Ryder just adjusted his hat and nudged his horse forward.

"We riding or standing around?" Rourke said and gave the order. The posse moved out. The canyon stretched ahead, the heat sinking into the rocks. Madsen was out there. And Ryder had a bad feeling he wasn't just running.

Chapter 7 – A Snake in the Posse

The land stretched before them in a long, rolling expanse of hard-packed dirt and scattered brush, broken only by the occasional jut of rock or skeletal remains of long-dead trees. The sun, climbing higher, burned down on their backs, turning the air thick and dry. A bad heat for chasing men. A worse heat for being chased. Ryder rode near the back, his eyes drifting between the trail and the men ahead of him. The canyon fight was still fresh in his mind. He could still hear the gunfire, still see Sam Upton's body crumpling to the dirt, the mess that had been his head pooling red beneath him.

That had been a bad shot, it had come from close in, the angle had been wrong for it to have come from up on the Canyon walls. Ryder had seen enough dead men to know what a bullet from above did to a man and what a bullet from beside him did. Sam's wound hadn't come from the canyon walls. It had come from within the posse.

That left three men who could have fired it.

Ethan Doyle. Young, reckless, excitable. He had emptied his gun as fast as his hands could work the hammer, shooting wild, putting more lead into dirt and stone than anything else. Ryder could believe he'd hit Sam by accident, but it would have meant turning, twisting his aim and he had been concentrating too much on sending lead towards Marsden.

Will Tanner. A quiet man, who watched more than he spoke, a ranch hand with no real reason to be involved in this fight, yet here he was. Ryder had seen how he handled his rifle back in the canyon. Hadn't fired when he should have, he had been watching more than shooting – but that didn't make a man a killer.

Then there was Nathan Briggs, the ex-cavalry scout. Full of pride, full of resentment, he wanted to lead but couldn't quite get the men to follow. Ryder could feel the heat coming off him every time their eyes met. One of them had put Sam Upton in the ground, and Ryder meant to find out which.

By midmorning, Nathan led them to a watering hole, a small, shallow basin fed by a thin stream, the surface clouded with silt where horses had disturbed the water. Ryder took in the scene as they reined up. Hoofprints everywhere.

Nathan swung down from his horse, gesturing with satisfaction. "See that?" He looked to Rourke, triumphant. "They stopped here. Which means I've got them dead on."

Wyatt Steele

Ryder remained in his saddle, his fingers loose on the reins. It didn't take a tracker to see the prints. A half-blind man could've followed them this far. Still, Nathan was basking in it, his shoulders drawn back, his chin high. Will Tanner stood near him, a satisfied smirk playing at his lips. Ethan, still eager to fit in, was nodding along, shifting in his saddle like he wanted to be anywhere but next to Ryder.

Ryder said nothing. He just swung off his horse, leading Sparks toward the water, watching the way the land shaped itself around them. A man could lay an ambush here easy if he knew how. But it looked like Madsen and his gang had moved fast, stopping only long enough to rest their horses. Texas Bill had also stayed in the saddle. He caught Ryder's eye, quirking a brow, it seems he saw the danger too.

Nathan, still riding high on himself, turned to Rourke. "I say we press on before they get too far ahead."

Ryder exhaled through his nose, adjusting his hat. They'd already lost time burying Sam. Madsen had a few hours on them now. And if Ryder knew anything about that bastard, it was that he didn't just run, he set traps. Masden would want the Posse off his tail, and sure enough, twenty minutes down the trail, the first sign of trouble showed itself. The hoofprints split.

Ryder – Gone To Hell

Some of Madsen's men had veered left, cutting through a narrow ridge leading back toward the low scrub hills. The main trail continued ahead, following the easier path deeper into the canyonlands. Ryder pulled up, his gaze tracing the split paths. Madsen was too smart to lead a straight chase. This was deliberate. A split trail meant one of two things, a trap ahead or an ambush behind.

Ryder urged his horse forward. "Rourke."

The sheriff pulled up alongside him. "What?"

Ryder pointed toward the second trail. "Madsen split his men. We keep on the main path, and we're blind to whatever's coming up behind us."

Nathan scoffed. "Or maybe some of them just drifted, and you're looking for trouble where there ain't any."

"Madsen doesn't run sloppy." Ryder didn't look at him. "You don't split a gang when you're fleeing for your life. You do it when you've got a plan."

"Or when you're trying to shake your tail," Nathan shot back.

Ryder ignored him and kept his eyes on Rourke. "I've seen him do this before. If we push on without being careful, he'll have men swinging back round and putting bullets in our backs before we even know they're there."

Rourke's jaw tightened. He was remembering the canyon. Remembering how Ryder had warned them and how right he'd been. "You think he's circling?"

"I think if we don't stop and find out, we're gonna get picked off one by one," Ryder said.

Rourke considered it, he wasn't a fool, but he was cautious. He'd already lost a man and he wasn't about to lose another. "What do you suggest?"

Ryder took one last look at the split trails, then turned back. "We find high ground. Somewhere secure. We wait. If they're coming for us, they'll show themselves soon enough."

Nathan let out a short laugh. "And while we're sitting there twiddling our thumbs, Madsen is getting farther away. That's your great plan?"

Ryder finally turned to him, slow and deliberate. "You got a better one?"

Nathan's mouth twitched, but no words came.

Rourke's gaze slid between the two men before finally settling on Nathan. "You led us into that canyon without a second thought. I ain't making the same mistake twice. We take Ryder's suggestion."

Nathan went rigid. For the first time since they'd set out, he looked like he might actually snap. His jaw clenched, his nostrils flared, and for a moment, Ryder thought he might open his mouth and say something he'd regret.

But Will Tanner put a hand on Nathan's arm. "Let it go," he muttered.

Nathan held his breath, then let it out slow, forcing his shoulders to relax. "Fine," he said through gritted teeth.

But Ryder didn't miss the way his hand hovered a little too long near his belt. They'd found a snake in the posse, now, all that was left was to watch where it struck.

They turned away from the trail, veering off the clean path of hoofprints Madsen had left them, and started climbing. The land grew harsher as they rode, the ground breaking into jagged outcroppings of sunbaked stone, patches of dry brush rattling in the wind. The higher they went, the heavier the heat pressed down. Ryder could feel the resentment building behind him, thick as the dust kicked up by their horses. They didn't like this.

Nathan rode with his reins tight in his hands, his entire posture wound up with anger, barely keeping his frustration from boiling over. It was obvious in the way his horse moved beneath him, sensing its rider's mood. Will Tanner, riding beside him, wasn't much different; his expression was dark, and his mouth was set in a thin line. Even Ethan Doyle, who had spent most of the ride trying to find his place among them, was looking uneasy, though it was more from not wanting to be in the minority than any real conviction.

They thought they were losing Madsen. They thought Ryder's caution was cowardice. No one said it outright, but he could feel it in their silence, in the sidelong looks, in the muttered words passed between them. Tom Calder had kept his thoughts to himself, but even he was clearly impatient. He had lost a brother to Madsen and didn't want to lose the trail along with him.

Only Rourke seemed steady, sticking to Ryder's side, keeping his jaw locked tight, ignoring the brewing resentment around them. They reached higher ground after an hour's climb, pulling up their horses as the rocky outcrop flattened out into a small ridge. The ground was uneven, cracked from years under the punishing sun, but from here, they had a clear view of the land stretching below them. The trail they had abandoned twisted through the basin far beneath, disappearing into the rising hills where Madsen and his men had vanished.

The others dismounted, restless, already murmuring amongst themselves. Nathan was furious, pacing near the edge of the ridge, his boots grinding against stone. "This is a waste of time," he muttered. "We're sitting up here while they're riding free."

Will stepped up beside him, shaking his head. "Even if they were coming behind us, we could've taken them," he said, frustration clear in his voice. "Hell, we had the numbers."

Ethan shifted uncomfortably, clearly not wanting to speak up but not disagreeing either. "Feels like we're just watching the dust settle."

"Enough," Rourke said, his voice carrying. "We'll know soon if we made the right call."

Nathan scoffed, shaking his head as he turned away. Ryder didn't bother looking at him. He pulled his saddlebags loose, reaching inside until his fingers closed around cold brass and worn leather. He lifted the spyglass to his eye, steadying his arm against his knee as he swept his gaze across the landscape below. The desert stretched wide, rolling in waves of dry earth and sun-bleached rock, the wind kicking up thin spirals of dust along the horizon. For a moment, there was nothing but the vast emptiness of the land. Then he saw them.

Seven riders moved along the path they had just abandoned, moving carefully, keeping their distance. They were trailing the posse. Had been shadowing them. Ryder

Wyatt Steele

watched them a moment longer, tracking their movement, watching the way they kept themselves half-hidden, cautious. Then, without a word, he handed the spyglass to Rourke. The sheriff took it, adjusting the focus as he lifted it to his eye. The posse had gone dead silent, the sound of wind and the distant rustling of dry brush the only thing left as Rourke watched the five men below.

Then he lowered the spyglass, exhaling through his nose, his face hard. "They were following us," he muttered.

Nathan, who had been pacing just moments ago, stopped in his tracks. Ethan's face paled. Will said nothing. Below them, the outlaws must have realized they'd been spotted. Ryder watched as they pulled up short, their heads tilting upward toward the ridge, their body language shifting from quiet pursuit to wary hesitation. They weren't about to make an attack now, not against high ground. Instead, Ryder watched as they veered off, their horses kicking up dust as they turned, riding away from the ridge and picking up the trail that Madsen had taken. The posse stayed quiet, watching them go.

Then Texas Bill let out a slow breath and gave Ryder a grin. "Hell," he muttered, shaking his head. "I reckon you just kept me in one piece, cowboy."

Ryder just watched the retreating figures disappear into the hills. He didn't say a word. He didn't have to. Because now, they hated him even more. Nathan, Will, and Ethan—they had resented him before, but now? Now, Ryder had been right. And that was worse than being wrong. Only Rourke and Texas were still on his side. The rest were just waiting for a reason to turn on him.

Wyatt Steele

Chapter 8 – The Night Before

The fire burned low and steady, the flames licking at the dry wood, sending up thin curls of smoke that drifted into the cooling air. The smell of burning mesquite mingled with the ever-present scent of dust and sweat, of worn leather and horses, of men who had been too long in the saddle chasing something that didn't want to be caught.

The posse had settled in for the night, but there was no ease in it. They sat around the fire, boots scuffing against the dirt, and the occasional pop of wood was the only thing breaking the silence.

Tension lay heavy between them, thick as the night itself.

Texas sat across from Ryder, rolling a cigarette with slow, deliberate fingers, his face unreadable in the firelight. He didn't say much, but then again, he didn't need to. He'd been watching the others the same way Ryder had, reading the way they moved, the way they avoided meeting Ryder's eye, the way Nathan and Will muttered low between themselves, heads bent together like conspirators. Ethan sat close to them, eager to belong, eager to find his place, even if it meant siding with the wrong men. Ryder didn't care, he'd been alone before.

Ryder – Gone To Hell

The fire crackled, sending up a brief spray of embers, and the wind shifted, rolling through the camp like a thing alive, carrying with it the scent of dry earth and old bones of the endless desert stretching out into the night. It was the kind of wind that unsettled men, made them glance over their shoulders, and made them think too hard about what might be waiting out there in the dark. Coyotes began their howling, the sound high and lonesome, a chorus rising in the distance. Somewhere far beyond the reach of their fire, Madsen was moving.

Ryder didn't know where, but he knew it sure as anything. That bastard wasn't asleep. Nathan shifted where he sat, rubbing at his hands, then stretched out his legs like he was trying to shake something off. The firelight caught on his face, and for a moment, Ryder saw something flicker across his expression. Frustration. Maybe something more.

"You really think they're out there?" Ethan asked suddenly, breaking the silence. His voice was tight, uncertain. "Madsen's men, I mean. You think they're coming after us?"

Nathan scoffed, leaning forward, his elbows resting on his knees. "Kid, if they were out there, we'd already know it."

Wyatt Steele

Ryder flicked his eyes toward him but didn't respond. Because Nathan was wrong. Madsen's men weren't reckless. They weren't like the wild gangs that tore through border towns, shooting up saloons and getting themselves killed in the process. They were disciplined. Smart. They followed orders. And Madsen wouldn't waste time taking potshots at them in the dark. If they were coming, they'd wait. They'd pick their moment.

Ethan chewed on that for a moment, then pulled his coat tighter around his shoulders. The night air had grown colder, the warmth of the day-long gone, replaced with the kind of chill that seeped into a man's bones if he let it.

Tom Calder sat with his back to a rock, silent, staring at the fire but seeing something else entirely. Probably his brother, bleeding out in the dirt, or maybe Madsen, still out there, still breathing when he shouldn't be. Rourke sat apart from them, head bowed, his face unreadable in the shifting light. He'd been watching Ryder all day, considering him. He hadn't taken Nathan's side, but he hadn't shut him down either. Rourke was a careful man. And careful men were the hardest to read.

The fire popped again, another ember floating into the night. Texas exhaled slowly, rolling the cigarette between his fingers before tucking it between his lips and lighting it. He took a drag, then exhaled, the smoke curling like a ghost in the darkness.

He looked at Ryder. "Think they'll come?"

Ryder shrugged. "If they're smart, they already are."

That earned a grunt from Texas, and the smirk that followed was almost amused. "You got a way of making a man sleep easy, cowboy."

Ryder didn't respond. Instead, he tipped his hat down slightly, leaning back against his saddle, one hand resting easily against the butt of his gun. The wind picked up again, rattling the dry brush, carrying the coyotes' song further across the empty land. Somewhere out there, in the blackness of the desert, Madsen was waiting. And Ryder knew one thing for certain. When morning came, they'd be closer to hell than they were now.

At Dawn, They Set Out. The sky was still bruised with the last traces of night when they broke camp; the fire was reduced to nothing but a bed of smoldering embers. The cold lingered in the air, biting at fingers and stiffening joints as they saddled their horses, their breath curling in the weak morning light.

Nathan was the first to mount up, riding out ahead before anyone else was even in the saddle. He'd found the trail again, or at least that's what he claimed. His posture was different now; his back was straighter, and his movements were more assured, like a man who had finally proven something to himself. The doubt and anger from the night before had settled into something closer to triumph.

He had found the way. He was leading them now. And he meant to make damn sure everyone knew it. Ryder watched him from beneath the brim of his hat, adjusting his saddle before swinging up onto Sparks's back. He didn't say a word. Didn't argue. Didn't challenge the tracking. It wasn't worth it. Instead, he fell into line near Texas and Rourke, keeping his eyes on the ground, watching the land change as they rode. The canyons were behind them now, the steep rock walls giving way to a wider, more open stretch of country. But that didn't mean they were safer.

The terrain shifted as the morning wore on, hard-packed dirt giving way to cracked scrubland, the kind of place where a man could ride for miles without seeing so much as a bird. The heat had yet to settle, but it was coming. The sun rose slowly and relentlessly, creeping toward its midday burn. Nathan rode ahead, guiding them along the deep tracks left behind by

Madsen's gang. The prints were clear, stamped deep in the dirt, and easy enough for anyone to follow. But Nathan held himself like a man reading some secret message in them, like every scuff and hoof mark was speaking only to him.

Behind him, Will rode close, quiet but watching everything. Ethan lingered near them, his eyes flicking between Ryder and Nathan, torn between the divide that had been growing since the canyon. Ryder kept his distance, letting the rhythm of his horse carry him forward, listening to the way the land settled, the way the wind shifted. Something about this still felt wrong. The trail was too easy. Madsen was too smart for that. They were riding fast, following a line that had been left clear as day, but Ryder couldn't shake the feeling that they weren't just following a trail. They were being led.

Texas must have felt it too because, after a while, he leaned over slightly in the saddle, voice low. "You trust him?"

Ryder didn't look at him. "No."

Texas let out a slow breath through his nose, adjusting his grip on the reins. "Yeah," he muttered, "didn't think so."

Rourke, riding just ahead of them, kept his gaze on the trail, but Ryder could tell by the way his shoulders set that he was thinking the same thing. They pressed on, dust rising beneath their horses, the land stretching endlessly before them. The canyons were behind them. But the real danger was still ahead.

The sun hung high overhead, merciless and steady, burning down on the land as they rode toward the trading post. It was the kind of place a man expected to hear the bustle of voices, the hammering of a blacksmith working a stubborn shoe onto a horse's hoof, and the low murmur of traders haggling over prices.

Instead—nothing.

No movement.

No wagons in the yard. No horses tied to the hitching posts. The wind picked up, rattling the dry grass along the roadside and sending dust swirling up from the packed earth. A wooden sign swung on iron chains, creaking lazily as they approached, the paint peeling, the letters barely legible beneath years of sun and wind. Ryder felt it settle in his gut before they even reached the main yard. Something was wrong.

They slowed as they entered the trading post, boots tightening in stirrups, reins held taut. Hands drifted closer to holsters, fingers flexing over the worn grips of their guns.

Texas Bill was the first to speak, his voice low but firm. "I don't like this."

Ryder didn't answer.

Neither did Rourke.

Ryder – Gone To Hell

Because they all saw it at the same time.

The place looked deserted but not abandoned. There were still barrels stacked outside the general store. The barn doors were ajar, swaying slightly with the breeze as if someone had just passed through. The doors to the trading post itself were partway open, a curtain shifting in the still air.

And yet—no one.

Ryder eased back in the saddle, letting his eyes drift over the yard. The dirt was stirred up, hoof prints overlapping boot tracks, like men had passed through in a hurry. Too many tracks for just the trader and a few passing wagons.

Rourke's voice came low and steady. "Eyes open."

They dismounted, boots hitting the dirt with a heaviness that wasn't just weight. Ryder kept his hand near his Colt as he moved forward, his eyes flicking to the barn, then the open doors of the trading post. Tom Calder was already stepping toward the front of the store, his jaw clenched tight, his grief-worn face drawn with something unreadable. Nathan had one hand on his rifle, but his focus was on Ryder, not the buildings. Will and Ethan hung back slightly, unsure, waiting to see what the others did.

Wyatt Steele

Texas Bill nudged a half-empty water barrel with his boot, watching it rock slightly, the water inside sloshing against the sides. "Somebody was here."

Ryder already knew it. But somebody wasn't here anymore.

A sound buzzed low through the air—the slow, steady drone of flies. Ryder turned his head toward the porch of the trading post. That's when he saw him. A man lay face down in the dirt, his arms stretched out, his fingers curled in the dust like he'd been crawling before he died. His shirt was dark with blood, soaked through at the stomach and spreading outward in thick, drying patches. Flies clustered at the wound, swarming in lazy circles, the sound of their wings thick in the empty yard.

For a long moment, nobody spoke. Then Ethan let out a slow, shaky breath. "Jesus."

Rourke stepped forward first, his boots kicking up small puffs of dust as he approached the body. He crouched down, rolling the man over onto his back. The trader's face was pale, his mouth slightly open, his eyes vacant and unseeing.

Texas rubbed at his jaw, shaking his head. "Damn."

Ryder crouched beside the body, the smell of death thick in the warm air, mixing with the dust that swirled at his boots. The trader lay stiff and still, his arms sprawled out like he'd tried to crawl away from whatever hell had found him. His shirt was black with dried blood, the stain spreading outward in thick, uneven patches. Ryder's eyes traced the ground around him—no weapon, no sign he'd had a fighting chance. Just the lifeless stretch of desert, the emptiness of a place that should have been bustling with people, and the body of a man who'd been left behind. And written on the door of a barn not far away in the man's blood was one word, scrawled in dark, drying streaks.

His name.

RYDER.

Written in the man's blood. For a long moment, no one said a damn thing. The wind moved through the buildings, whispering through the empty spaces where life should have been. The old barn doors groaned, swaying on their hinges. Overhead, a buzzard let out a sharp, hungry cry, circling low in the sky.

Rourke was the first to break the silence. He let out a slow breath, rubbing at his temple like this was all starting to make sense in the worst possible way. "Well," he muttered, shaking his head, "looks like this got personal."

Nathan shifted beside him, his gaze flicking toward Ryder. There was something in that look—not just resentment, but suspicion. Will Tanner stood a few feet away, arms crossed, his face unreadable. Ethan, still too young to know any better, looked nervous as hell, his fingers twitching slightly where they rested near his belt.

Tom Calder was watching Ryder too, his hand curled over the grip of his revolver, his jaw tight. "Why's he after you?" Tom asked, his voice sharp.

Ryder didn't answer right away. He let his eyes settle on the bloody letters, the message left there for them—for him. Finally, he stood, dusting his gloves against his coat before stepping off the porch.

"Ain't after me," he said at last.

He walked toward his horse, adjusting the saddle, his movements easy, unhurried like the weight of the message hadn't settled deep in his gut. "He just knows how to keep us chasing him. Like I said, I met him in Arizona, then joined the posse that tried to chase him down. I was in the saloon the night he shot the dealer, he knows my name."

"Yeah, you're not an easy man to forget, I guess," Rourke said running his eyes from Ryder's boots to his hat, "All six foot six of you," He let out another breath before stepping back from the body. He adjusted his hat, his face grim. "Well, then," he muttered. "Let's not keep him waiting."

"Maybe you know Masden a little better than you're letting on?" Nathan said suddenly, all eyes turned to him. "Masden had men in the crowd at the hanging, men who were helping him to escape. What's to say he doesn't have a man in this posse?"

"That was a hell of an accusation, Nathan, and you've nothing, I say, nothing to base it on," Rourke said, shutting him down.

But it was too late. Nathan had said it.

Chapter 9 – The Seeds of Doubt

The sun was high and merciless, burning down on their shoulders as the posse gathered near their horses, the weight of the trading post still heavy in the air. The wind had picked up slightly, rustling through the brittle brush, carrying the lingering stench of blood and dust. The body lay where they had left it, stiffening in the heat, the name RYDER still written in dried blood. They had seen worse in the past few days. But somehow, this was different. Madsen had left a message. And now, every man in the posse was wondering what it meant.

Wyatt Steele

Rourke turned toward Ryder, his expression unreadable, his voice even. "How the hell does Madsen know you're with me?"

It wasn't a challenge. Not yet. Just a question that needed answering. Ryder didn't hesitate. He met the sheriff's gaze, steady as ever. Lying wouldn't get him anywhere, and he wasn't in the business of explaining himself. "When I was drinking my coffee on the saloon porch, he looked me straight in the eyes as they put the noose over his head." Ryder adjusted his hat, squinting slightly against the glare of the sun. "He knew then."

Silence stretched between them, the weight of his words sinking in. It didn't sit right with the others.

Will let out a short, humorless laugh, shaking his head. "So, you're saying he just... knew you'd be part of the posse?"

Ryder shrugged. "Madsen's always been good at reading men. He probably figured the town would chase him. Figured I'd be part of it."

Will let out another short exhale through his nose, shaking his head as he looked over at Nathan, who gave him a knowing glance. No one spoke, but Ryder could feel the shift. It wasn't just curiosity anymore. It was doubt. He could see it in Ethan's uncertain expression, the way his fingers tapped against his thigh, shifting uncomfortably in the saddle. He saw it in

Ryder – Gone To Hell

Tom Calder's stiff posture, the way his grip had tightened ever so slightly on the reins. Nathan didn't bother hiding it.

His stare was sharp, his lips pressed into a thin, bitter line. "You ever wonder, Ryder?" Nathan finally said, his tone light but his meaning anything but. "What it is about you that makes men like Madsen remember your name?"

The words settled between them like a slow-burning fuse.

Rourke exhaled hard through his nose, adjusting his hat. "Enough," he said. "We move out."

The order was given, but the doubt didn't leave. And Ryder knew then—he wasn't just watching his back for Madsen's men anymore.

The wind had picked up, rolling through the sparse brush and rattling loose boards on the abandoned buildings. The stench of dried blood and sun-baked death still clung to the air, mingling with the dust kicked up by their restless horses. Ryder didn't care much about the way the others started watching him. Suspicion had settled thick over the posse like a storm brewing on the horizon. He could feel it. Ethan kept shifting in his saddle, Tom Calder's jaw had gone tight, and Nathan was clenching the reins like he wanted to break them in half.

Wyatt Steele

Nathan wasn't buying it. He pulled his horse a little closer, his posture stiff, his shoulders squared. "You were the one who tracked him before, right?" His voice was casual, but there was a sharp edge to it, like the blade of a knife just beneath the surface.

Ryder didn't react. Didn't turn his head. Didn't blink.

Nathan's eyes narrowed. He wanted a reaction. "If you're so damn good at it," he went on, "why'd you let him go last time?"

The words landed heavily in the silence that followed. The others were listening now. Ryder felt all of them watching him. He reached up, adjusting his hat, his voice easy, flat.

"He had the border at his back." He let his eyes drift to Nathan, slow and deliberate. "Wasn't worth chasing a man into Mexico when the law wouldn't follow."

Nathan scoffed, shaking his head. "Sounds like an excuse."

Ryder didn't blink. "Sounds like the truth."

The moment hung there, stretched tight. The kind of silence that meant something could break at any second.

Will Tanner leaned in slightly from where he sat in the saddle, his smirk growing. "You gonna let him talk to you like that, Nathan?"

His tone was light, but the intent wasn't. He was baiting him. Trying to get

Ryder – Gone To Hell

Nathan to take a swing. Trying to stir up trouble where there didn't need to be any. Ryder saw it for exactly what it was. And he didn't rise to it. Didn't shift. Didn't reach for his gun. Didn't even let his fingers twitch. Instead, he just stared at Nathan—long enough to make it a choice. Nathan's jaw tightened. His fingers curled around the reins. But he didn't move. Not yet. The air between them was thick and still, waiting.

Then Rourke sighed, loud and sharp. "Enough," he said, his voice carrying over them like a warning.

Nathan hesitated, his eyes still locked on Ryder. Then—slowly, stiffly—he pulled his horse back. But Ryder didn't miss the way his hand hovered near his belt just a second too long. And he knew—this wasn't over.

Texas Bill leaned against his saddle, arms crossed over his chest, watching the exchange with the air of a man who'd seen too many fights start this way. There was something almost amused in his expression, the corners of his mouth twitching like he was debating whether to say something or just let it all play out.

Nathan's horse stamped at the ground, sensing the tension, its muscles twitching beneath the leather of the reins. Nathan was still tight in the saddle, his jaw clenched, his hands flexing on the horn of his saddle like he was trying to keep himself from reaching for something else.

The air was thick with something unspoken but dangerous—a breath held too long, a trigger cocked but not pulled. Ethan Doyle shifted uneasily. His eyes darted from Ryder to Nathan, then to Will, as if trying to measure where he stood in all of this. He didn't have the same fire in him as the others. He was still young, still figuring out what kind of man he wanted to be. But he could feel the weight of the moment, the way it was shaping the lines between them.

And he didn't like it.

Tom Calder had been quiet this whole time, his hands loose on the reins, his expression unreadable. But now, he exhaled sharply as if he'd finally had enough. "None of this matters," Tom said, his voice cutting through the heat of the moment. "The bastard's still out there, and we're still riding after him. Or did everyone forget that?"

A beat of silence followed, the wind shifting through the brush, stirring the dust at their feet.

Rourke nodded once, his gaze sweeping over the group, his tone firm but final. "We keep moving. Madsen's ahead of us, and we're not losing any more time standing around talking."

It was a command, not a suggestion. Nathan hesitated for a second longer, his lips pressing into a thin, angry line. He cast one last glare at Ryder, but whatever fight he wanted to start—he swallowed it down. For now. Will Tanner, on the other hand, just smirked to himself, like a man who had just watched a good show and was looking forward to the next act.

There was a shift as they moved toward their horses, saddles creaking, dust kicking up beneath their boots. The posse mounted up, the brief moment of stillness breaking as the horses turned toward the open trail ahead. But things weren't the same anymore. The divide was there now, clear as the tracks they followed. Nathan and Will rode together, shoulders tight, their voices low and private. Ethan kept a little closer to them now, unsure but unwilling to be the one man standing alone. Tom Calder held his focus forward, his silence the only thing keeping him separate from the rift.

Texas rode alongside Ryder, giving him a sideways glance, his grin still lingering, but there was an edge to it now. "Hell of a thing, cowboy."

Ryder didn't reply. He just nudged his horse forward, eyes on the horizon, knowing that whatever trouble had started back there—It wasn't over yet.

The sun rode high and unrelenting as the posse pressed forward, their shadows stretching long against the hard-packed dirt. The land had widened again, stretching into rolling scrub and scattered rock, but it didn't feel open. Not to Ryder. He could feel the shift, a subtle change in the air, a change in the posse.

The canyon, the trading post, the name written in blood—none of it had settled right. It was sticking to them, weighing on their shoulders like a storm creeping over the horizon. Only this storm wasn't rolling in from the desert. It was right here in the saddle beside him. Nathan rode quiet, his posture stiff, his fingers flexing against the reins. He was still angry, still stewing, still waiting. Watching Ryder like he was expecting him to slip, expecting a mistake, expecting a reason to turn all that festering resentment into something solid.

Will Tanner wasn't angry, not like Nathan. His amusement was worse, the knowing little smirk that tugged at the corner of his mouth, the way he rode easy in the saddle like he'd already figured out the ending to this story. Like he could see exactly how the next few days were going to go, and he wasn't in any rush to stop it. Even Ethan, who had been neutral before, had started hanging back, unsure. He wasn't outright hostile, not yet. But Ryder had seen it before—the way a man could get caught between two sides, the way he could start convincing himself that stepping away from one was the same as choosing the other. That was how men got killed out here. The

Ryder – Gone To Hell

only two who hadn't changed were Texas and Rourke.

Texas stayed close, his horse never straying far from Ryder's, a silent vote of confidence. He hadn't said much, but Ryder didn't need words to know Texas had already picked a side. Rourke, though? Rourke was harder to read. The sheriff didn't give away much, but Ryder could tell he was watching. Watching Nathan. Watching Will. Watching how the air had changed between all of them. And he was keeping a tight grip on the reins. Because if Madsen wasn't the one to break them first—One of their own would be.

Wyatt Steele

Chapter 10 – A Desperate Gamble

The hills grew darker, the last traces of daylight fading behind the ridgelines, leaving only the silver glow of the moon spilling over jagged rock. The air, once thick with the heat of the day, began to cool, turning crisp with the kind of night chill that settled deep into a man's bones if he let it. The fire burned low and steady, its glow barely reaching beyond the gathered men, sending thin ribbons of smoke curling upward, lost in the endless sprawl of stars. It flickered weakly against the uneven stone surrounding them, throwing fleeting shadows across their faces, highlighting the hard lines and unspoken tension.

They had camped in a narrow depression between two ridges, a place that, on paper, offered some shelter from the wind but, in truth, left them penned in. Ryder wouldn't have picked it. Too many blind spots. Too easy to be trapped. But no one had asked him. No one was asking him much of anything these days. The ground was uneven, scattered with loose shale and patches of dry, scrubby grass. The hills, which had felt open and vast during the day, now seemed to close in tight, their jagged

Ryder – Gone To Hell

peaks forming a black silhouette against the sky.

The horses had been tethered on the other side of the ridge, near a thick patch of scrub and wind-warped mesquite trees. The brush offered some cover, but it also meant the animals were out of sight, too far for comfort. Ryder had wanted to say something. Had wanted to point out that they were better off keeping the horses in view, closer to the fire, where a man could see if someone came for them. But he hadn't. Because he already knew how that would go, so he'd kept his mouth shut and let them make their choices.

And now, as the wind shifted through the ridges, rustling through the brittle brush and carrying the high, lonely cry of a coyote, Ryder sat by the fire, watching the dark beyond its glow, waiting. Nathan kept his distance from Ryder, every movement stiff and resentful. Will Tanner was in better spirits, lounging near the fire and rolling a cigarette with easy fingers, like he had nowhere else to be and nothing better to do. He hadn't said much, but his smirk had never quite faded. Ethan sat hunched near the fire, rubbing his hands together and throwing occasional glances at Nathan and Will as if he wasn't sure whose side he was supposed to be on. Tom Calder sat apart from the others, cleaning his gun in silence.

Wyatt Steele

Texas Bill muttered a few words under his breath about the cold settling into his damn bones, but even he didn't have much to say.

And Rourke? The Sheriff just sat there, staring into the flames like he was reading the future in the embers. Ryder kept his eyes on the darkness beyond the firelight. Because something felt off. He didn't know if it was Madsen's men out there or just the tension in the camp making his skin itch. But the weight in his gut told him something was coming.

Then it happened.

The first shot cracked through the darkness, shattering the quiet and echoing hard off the canyon walls like a roll of thunder.

A second followed.

A third.

Then—chaos.

Before anyone could react, the sound of hoofbeats exploded from the other side of the ridge. The horses screamed and bolted, the sound of their hooves pounding against the hard-packed ground, the sharp clatter of kicked-up stones tumbling down the slope. The commotion was loud and wild, sending dust and broken scrub flying as the animals tore free and ran blindly into the night.

For a split second, it sounded like riders coming straight for them.

Ethan panicked at first. He dove for cover, pulling his gun and firing blindly into the dark. The shots cracked loudly, sending sparks off a rock outcrop. Ryder moved fast, grabbing him by the arm, stopping him before he emptied his gun. "Don't shoot at something you can't see!" His voice was low and firm. "Our damned horses are over there!"

Ethan froze, breathing hard, realization dawning just as the hoofbeats started to fade. The others had scrambled to cover, crouched behind rocks, weapons drawn, straining to see through the dark.

Nathan had his rifle shouldered, his breath heavy. "Did you see anything?"

Rourke was already moving, stepping out from the fire's glow, his eyes narrowing as he scanned the ridge. "Spread out. But stay close."

They moved cautiously, fanning out, eyes sweeping across the rocks and the brush, searching for movement.

But there was nothing.

No figures shifting in the dark.

No gunmen sneaking through the brush.

Just the faint dust cloud left in the wake of their runaway horses and the last echo of the shots rolling off the hills.

Then—silence. A deep, unnatural quiet settled over the camp, heavy and suffocating.

Their horses were gone.

Wyatt Steele

Nathan was the first to move, striding toward where the horses had been tethered, his boots kicking up dust as he reached down and snatched at a loose length of rope. It was cleanly sliced, not frayed, not chewed—cut with purpose. "Son of a bitch!" he growled, throwing the rope. "They cut them loose!"

Rourke muttered something under his breath, his jaw tight as he followed Nathan, scanning the ground. Ethan wasn't far behind, standing wide-eyed and pale, shifting his weight like he wanted to do something but had no idea what.

"They were right there," Ethan said, almost disbelieving. His voice was tight, edged with panic. "How the hell did someone get that close?"

Tom Calder was moving along the edge of the ridge, scanning the darkness, his fingers flexing around the grip of his revolver. His mouth was set in a thin line, his frustration simmering beneath the surface. "Damn bastards got us right where they want us," he muttered.

Will Tanner wasn't quiet about his thoughts. He stormed up beside Nathan, eyes blazing, his voice sharp and sure. "This was Madsen. You know it was. Sneakin' in, waitin' till we were sittin' pretty, then cuttin' us off, leavin' us marooned out here like jackasses." He spat into the dirt, shaking his head. "Hell, we might as well start diggin' our own graves while we're at it."

Texas swore under his breath and took a long drag from his cigarette, exhaling slowly, his eyes sweeping over the broken tether ropes. "Damn good way to make sure we don't keep after him."

Rourke wasn't saying much, but Ryder could see the way his hands clenched into fists at his sides. This wasn't just bad. It was a goddamn disaster. They were stranded. Deep in the desert, miles from any town, with no horses and no way to make up lost ground. Ryder had seen men die slowly out here, not from gunshots, not from fights, but from the desert itself. It didn't take much. Just a few too many miles under the sun. Just a little less water than a man thought he needed. Just a stretch of bad luck. And right now? Luck wasn't on their side.

Will and Nathan had rebuilt the fire, their movements sharp and angry, snapping dry branches in half and tossing them into the flames as if breaking something would settle the fury boiling beneath their skin. The fire burned low and sullen, throwing restless shadows across the jagged rock walls that boxed them in. No one was going back to sleep tonight.

Wyatt Steele

Nathan was still cursing, pacing near the ruined tether lines, his boots kicking up dust. "Son of a bitch." His voice had a raw edge to it, strained from a mix of rage and exhaustion.

Rourke ran a hand down his face, sighing, before squaring his shoulders and turning to the men. His voice was calm but firm, leaving no room for argument. "Check what you've got. Make sure your pieces are loaded. We're gonna have to carry what we need, and the rest, we leave."

More curses followed.

Tom Calder muttered something under his breath as he knelt by his saddlebags, sorting through supplies that now felt heavier than they had before. Texas didn't say much, but Ryder caught the way his mouth pulled tight as he tossed a canteen from one hand to the other, weighing how much water he had. Ethan, still shaken, checked his gun with nervous fingers, fumbling with the cylinder before snapping it shut.

Nathan, though, wasn't having it. He spun toward Rourke, eyes flashing. "Like hell I'm leaving my gear! That saddle's new. Do you know how much that damn thing cost me? I ain't leaving it behind."

Rourke barely looked at him. "Then carry it."

Nathan's nostrils flared, and his fists clenched at his sides. "That's bullshit,

Ryder – Gone To Hell

Sheriff! This whole thing is bullshit! We should've rode on, but no, we had to stop; we had to play things safe." He jabbed a finger toward Ryder. "And now, we're stranded in the middle of goddamn nowhere!"

Silence.

Everyone was watching now.

Will Tanner leaned back on his heels, arms crossed, his smirk barely contained. He was enjoying this, waiting for the fuse to catch fire.

Rourke took a slow breath, his patience worn to the bone. "You want the saddle, Nathan?" His voice was quiet now, more dangerous for it. "Then carry it. On your damn back."

Nathan looked ready to explode. For a second, Ryder thought he was gonna do something stupid. But something in Rourke's stare must have cut through whatever rage was burning in him because Nathan let out a breath, turned, and stomped toward the fire. He didn't touch his saddle, but he didn't let go of his anger either. The splintering of the posse was happening fast. And it was getting worse by the hour.

Wyatt Steele

The first light of dawn began to sneak over the hills, and while the others argued, their voices rose and fell like the wind sweeping through the canyon; Ryder moved away from the fire, away from the frayed nerves and flaring tempers. He walked toward the place where their horses had been tethered, his boots crunching softly over loose shale and dry earth. He wasn't looking for where they had gone. He already knew that was a lost cause until daylight. He was looking for why.

Ryder stayed crouched near the scattered dirt and severed tethers, fingers running through the loose grit, his mind working through what had just happened. The only tracks he could see were the ones left behind by their spooked horses, deep impressions where hooves had dug in before bolting. The ground was a mess of churned-up dust and overlapping prints, the kind of wild scattering that happened when animals fled in fear. But that was it. No boot tracks. No sign of anyone slipping into the camp to cut the tethers, just the chaos left behind once the damage had already been done. This wasn't a hit-and-run by outlaws, it was a setup, a deliberate, calculated move.

Ryder had spent too many years tracking both men and animals, and he knew no one had entered their camp the previous night. Someone had set this up. Someone had planned for them to be on foot.

Ryder – Gone To Hell

And that meant one thing. Madsen wasn't the only enemy out here.

Then he found something else.

A patch of darker earth, the smell of smoke still faint in the cooling night air. Ryder moved past the cut tethers, stepping carefully through the scrub, and there— hidden behind a thorny mesquite bush—he found it. A burnt-out fire ground into the dirt. Still warm. It had been stamped out fast, the embers crushed beneath a boot like someone had tried to erase the evidence before slipping away into the night. But they'd missed something. Spent cartridges. Ryder reached down, picking one up, rolling it between his fingers. The brass was still warm to the touch, tarnished slightly from the heat. He turned it over, feeling the weight of the casing, the jagged edge where the round had discharged. This wasn't an ambush, it wasn't Madsen's men sneaking into the camp and cutting loose the horses while they slept, someone had built this fire, thrown bullets into the flames, and let the heat cook them off, firing them into the air like gunshots. They'd cut the tethers and then slipped back into the camp, waiting for the fire to do its work.

And it had worked. Everyone was convinced they had been attacked during the night, that Masden's men had fired the shots and sent their horses off into the night. Ryder exhaled slowly, rubbing his thumb along the ridge of the casing, his mind turning over the pieces, lining them up. Somebody wanted them stranded, on foot and vulnerable, but which one was it? Ryder straightened, scanning the camp, his eyes moving over the men one by one.

Nathan was pacing furiously, his boots grinding into the dirt, his hands clenching and unclenching at his sides. "They could be anywhere by now!" His voice was sharp, bitter. "We'll never catch them up on foot!"

Will was standing just behind him, arms crossed over his chest, shaking his head slightly as if the whole thing was just a little too amusing.

Rourke stood off to the side, rubbing his jaw, his eyes flicking between the fire and the darkness beyond. He was thinking, always thinking.

Texas was muttering, more to himself than anyone else, shaking his head as he adjusted his gun belt. "Should've known better than to sleep easy."

Ethan looked half-sick, shifting on his feet like he wanted to speak but didn't know how.

Ryder watched them all.

And he knew.

Knew they weren't just outnumbered by Madsen's gang. Knew that by morning, this posse was going to tear itself apart. He also knew that when his horse eventually came back—and she would, because she always did, they were going to blame him. And if he wasn't careful, he'd be the next one dead in the dirt.

Ryder could feel it in the way the silences stretched too long, in the way every man seemed a little more on edge, the posse was breaking apart. Ryder needed an ally. But who? The weight of the night's events—losing their horses, losing their advantage—had settled into their bones, and doubt was creeping in like a sickness. Rourke had backed him before, but now? His authority had taken a hard hit. Losing their horses had shaken the men's trust in him. A posse was only as strong as its leader. And a leader without control was just another man trying to keep order in a crumbling world.

Ryder wasn't stupid. If he wanted to get out of this alive, he needed someone on his side.

Ethan was too green, too easily swayed. The kid had spent the whole night flinching at shadows, shifting uncomfortably between Nathan and Will, his eyes darting every time someone raised their voice. He was still young enough to be looking for direction—and he'd take it from whoever spoke the loudest. Tom Calder was too caught up in his own vengeance. He

Wyatt Steele

wasn't here to think; he was here to put a bullet in Madsen's head. As far as he was concerned, everything else was secondary.

Will? Absolutely not. The man had been poking at Nathan since the start, nudging him closer and closer to doing something reckless. Will liked watching things break—whether it was people or plans, it didn't seem to matter much to him.

Nathan? Hell no. Nathan already wanted a fight, and because of the way things were going, he'd get one before long.

That left Texas. Ryder flicked a glance toward him. The old gun hand was sitting on a flat rock near the fire, rolling a cigarette between his fingers, his face unreadable. Texas wasn't afraid to call things how he saw them. And most importantly—Texas wasn't stupid. If Ryder was going to find one man in this camp who still had a lick of sense left in him, it was going to be him. And with the way things were turning, Ryder was going to need him before this was over.

Ryder moved through the camp, slow and quiet, weaving past bedrolls and packs strewn haphazardly after the chaos. He wasn't interested in the others—not right now. He found Texas near the edge of camp, crouched beside his saddle, packing his bags with a slow, deliberate motion. Not rushed, not panicked, just thinking.

Texas wasn't a man to act without weighing his options first. That was why

Ryder – Gone To Hell

Ryder had come to him. Ryder crouched down beside him, his movements careful, calculated, no sudden gestures, he needed Texas to listen before he reacted. He reached into his coat and pulled out the spent cartridge from the fire, rolling it once between his fingers before opening his palm and holding it out. The brass caught a sliver of firelight, a dull shine against the dirt-streaked calluses of his hand.

"These were in a small fire," Ryder said, keeping his voice low. "On the other side of the horses."

Texas stilled, his hand pausing on the strap of his saddlebag. Then, slowly, he looked at Ryder. Not at the cartridge first—at him. Then he dropped his gaze, studying the round in Ryder's palm. For a long moment, he said nothing. Then he let out a slow breath through his nose and rubbed at his jaw. "Son of a bitch." He reached for the cartridge, rolling it between his thick fingers, feeling its weight. "This was the gunshots?"

Ryder nodded. "Someone set the fire, threw the rounds in, let the heat cook 'em off." He gestured vaguely toward the dark beyond camp. "Made it sound like we were under fire."

Texas exhaled through his teeth, shaking his head. "That's some tricky work."

Ryder studied him, watching the way his brow furrowed, the way his lips pressed together in a thin line as he turned the casing over again and again.

Then Texas glanced up, his gaze sharp. "Show me."

Ryder shook his head. "We walk over there together, we tip our hand. Whoever did this will know we're onto 'em."

Texas considered that. He wasn't a man prone to rash decisions. He didn't speak just to fill silence, didn't act without thought. Ryder could see the gears turning behind his eyes, weighing the truth of it. Then—just for a fraction of a second—his gaze flicked toward Nathan. Just a quick glance. But it was there. And Ryder saw it. Texas didn't say anything. He didn't have to. And for the first time since the horses bolted, Ryder felt a little less alone.

Ryder was about to say more, was about to warn Texas to keep his eyes open, to watch his back because something wasn't right in this camp. But before the words left his mouth, he felt it—a shift in the air. A sound, faint at first, carried on the wind. A single set of hooves on packed dirt, the rhythm was steady, unhurried, not the wild scatter of a spooked animal, not the chaotic retreat of a herd lost to the night. This was different. Ryder already knew what it was before he even turned his head. His horse had come back.

She stood just beyond the camp, a ghost in the early dawn light, her dun-colored coat blending against the shadows. Her ears flicked forward at the sound of voices, her nostrils flaring as she took in the camp. The cut tether still dangled from her head collar, frayed at the edges where the blade had done its work. She'd run when the others had. But she'd come back, just like Ryder knew she would. He stepped forward, slow and easy, keeping his voice low and steady as he spoke to her.

"That's a good girl, Sparks," he murmured, taking another step closer. She shifted slightly but didn't bolt, her body tense, waiting. Ryder reached into his coat pocket, his fingers closing around the dried apple slice he always carried for her. He held it out in his palm.

She lowered her head, sniffed at it, and then took it with a soft crunch, her nose nudging against his hand in quiet recognition. Tired. Dusty. But unharmed. He ran a hand along her neck, calming her, grounding himself in the familiar feel of her warm hide.

Then—the others rushed in. The sound of boots crunching hard against the dirt filled the air as the rest of the posse closed in, their faces lit with sudden, desperate hope.

Nathan was the first to step forward, his head snapping up toward the dark beyond the camp. "Where are the others?" His voice was sharp, demanding.

Ryder didn't answer because he didn't have to. The silence that followed spoke for itself. The hope in their faces faded, twisting into something harder, something meaner.

Texas sighed, rubbing his temple. "Damn."

Ethan's mouth opened, then closed, his expression crumpling. "They're not coming back, are they?"

"Not unless someone brings them back," Rourke said grimly, his eyes already scanning the ground, thinking ahead.

But Nathan wasn't interested in thinking ahead. He was already moving toward Ryder's horse, his frustration boiling over into something uglier.

"We need that horse to carry our gear," Nathan said, his voice flat, leaving no room for argument.

Ryder turned, his grip tightening on the reins. "She's mine."

Nathan didn't hesitate. Didn't blink. "Not anymore."

Before Ryder could react, Nathan leveled his gun at him, the camp went dead silent, every man froze where he stood. The fire crackled quietly, oblivious to the tension pressing in around it. Ryder's body was coiled tight, his muscles were tense, and his breath was slow and measured. His hand hovered near his own gun, but he didn't draw, not yet.

Nathan's eyes were hard as stone. "Hand that horse to Ethan, cowboy. This ain't up for discussion."

For a long moment, no one moved. Then, reluctantly, Ryder stepped back. He had no choice. Ethan moved in, not meeting his eyes, and took hold of the cut tether, and led her away.

Nathan still had the gun pointed at Ryder; Ryder stared him down, fury simmering beneath his skin.

Nathan smirked, thinking he'd won something. He turned and gestured to the others. "Get the saddles. Strap everything to her." And just like that, his horse was taken from him.

The men lashed every saddle and pack they could onto Ryder's buckskin, piling the weight high, turning her into nothing more than a beast of burden. Ryder's fists clenched at his sides, his breath tight, his body screaming for him to act.

Then—a hand on his arm.

Texas.

His grip was firm, steady. Ryder turned toward him, his rage barely contained. Texas met his gaze, his voice low, calm. A warning. A promise. "Bide your time, cowboy."

Ryder didn't answer. Because he knew Texas was right. And because one way or another, he was going to get his damn horseback.

Rourke finally spoke up, his voice cutting through the tension like a blade. "Enough. We follow the trail the horses left last night. We track 'em down."

No one liked it. But no one had a better idea. Nathan stood beside Ryder's horse, adjusting the straps like he had some right to her. Will stood nearby, watching Ryder, that same damn smirk on his face. Ethan still looked sick, like he wasn't sure whether to be angry or afraid. Ryder cast one last glance at his buckskin, weighed down under too much gear.

She was his.

She always had been.

And when he got her back—and he would—

He'd be settling some scores along with it.

Chapter 11 – A Tense March Under the Rising Sun

The sun barely touched the horizon when they set out, but already, the heat was pressing down, thick and unrelenting. The desert air was bone-dry, the kind that stole the sweat off a man's skin before it had a chance to cool him down. They moved in silence, the only sounds the crunch of boots against dry earth, the creak of leather, and the steady rasp of breath from men who had already had too much of one another.

Nathan led Ryder's buckskin, his grip tight on the reins, jaw set like a man who wanted to remind everyone that, for now, he was in control. The saddle, the packs, all their gear—it was lashed onto the mare's back, weighing her down like a pack mule.

Ryder walked at the rear, his eyes sweeping the ground, the land, the men ahead of him. The hoofprints of their missing horses stretched out before them, a faint, meandering trail etched into the dust, cutting through the scrub and over rocky patches. The animals had bolted hard, but they weren't wild—they had stayed together through the night.

At least so far.

Wyatt Steele

Ryder didn't like the way the trail twisted ahead, the way the heat was already pulling mirages up from the earth, shimmering waves distorting the horizon, making distances seem closer, and the land seem more treacherous. Nobody talked much. Nobody wanted to. The air was heavy, sullen, thick with frustration, exhaustion, and unspoken accusations. Every man was lost in his own thoughts.

Tom Calder walked a few steps ahead of Ryder, his hat pulled low, shoulders stiff. His brother's killer was still out there, and every wasted hour gnawed at him like a blade pressed too tight against the skin. Ethan lagged near the middle of the group, eyes darting from Nathan to Will, then to Ryder, like he was trying to figure out where the next explosion was coming from. Will, for his part, moved easy, unhurried, a man enjoying the friction, watching the cracks spread through the group like they were just another card game he was betting on. Texas walked beside Ryder, quiet, thoughtful. They were the only two who seemed to be watching the land as much as they were watching the men.

Ahead, Nathan muttered something under his breath and tugged a little harder on the reins of Ryder's horse. Ryder exhaled slowly. The day had barely started, and it already felt like it had stretched too long.

Ryder – Gone To Hell

And he had a feeling it was only going to get worse.

The heat was climbing fast, and with every mile they walked, the land seemed to stretch farther ahead, unchanging, merciless. The trail was still clear—a string of hoofprints etched into the hard-packed dirt, stretching like a winding thread toward the horizon. Then, after a few more miles, the signs changed.

Nathan was the first to pull up short. "Hold up."

The rest of the posse slowed, adjusting their packs and wiping sweat from their brows. Even the air felt different here, the ground ahead scattered with a mess of churned-up dirt and overlapping tracks. The horses had slowed here. Come together, hesitated.

Ryder walked forward, his gaze sweeping over the ground, his body moving on instinct, reading the land like a man who had spent a lifetime chasing trails. He crouched, running his fingers through the dry earth, letting the loose grit slip between his fingers. The prints were still deep, pressed hard into the dirt from the weight of frightened, running animals. But there was something different now—a shift in their pattern.

He traced the shape of a hoofprint with his fingertip, following the way it turned slightly, the way the weight changed. "So far," he muttered, mostly to himself, "they stayed together."

It made sense. A panicked herd would stick to the group, moving in one mass until they either tired or felt safe. But something had happened here.

They had stopped. Not all at once, not in a frenzy—but as if they had decided to. The hoofprints ahead weren't wild anymore. They were calmer, something had made them pause. Ryder stood slowly, brushing the dust from his hands, the others were watching him now.

"What do you see?" Rourke asked.

"Something changed," Ryder said, his voice even. "They stopped running."

Will scoffed, adjusting his pack. "Great. That means they can't be far."

Ryder ignored him, something wasn't adding up. And as he looked closer at the ground, he found the reason why. The tracks ahead didn't just show a halt—they showed a decision. Ryder took a few slow steps forward, his eyes scanning the dirt, his mind mapping the movements the horses had made. Then he saw it.

The herd hadn't stayed together. The main group of horses had continued west, their tracks still pressed in hard, still moving at a steady trot. But two had broken away. He followed the prints carefully, noting the subtle difference in the weight and the way the dirt had shifted beneath them. These two hadn't bolted blindly. They had slowed down. Deliberate, careful steps. They had paused, standing for a moment, considering—before veering north. Ryder exhaled through his nose, glancing up toward the ridge in the distance. They weren't just lost animals. Something had pulled them in that direction, and they were moving slower than the horses that had gone west.

"Well?" Nathan asked impatiently, kicking at a rock with his boot.

Ryder straightened. "The herd kept moving west," he said slowly. "But two of 'em broke off here. Went north."

Nathan frowned, stepping forward. "You sure?"

Ryder nodded toward the prints. "See for yourself."

Nathan squinted at the ground but didn't respond.

Texas was already watching Ryder, thoughtful. "And?"

Ryder hesitated, his eyes flicking between the two trails. Then he said, "I think we should follow the two."

Nathan let out a short, bitter laugh. "You want to follow two horses instead of six?"

Ryder didn't answer right away. He just looked at the hoofprints again; these were moving slower, and they'd got more chance of catching them up.

Ryder stood slowly, dusting his hands off, and moved toward Texas. He kept his voice low. "They won't listen to me, but they might listen to you."

Texas turned, his eyes narrowing slightly as he glanced at Ryder, then back at the trail. "You sure?"

Ryder nodded. "Best chance we got."

Texas considered it, exhaled slowly, and then set his jaw. And made his choice.

Texas stopped walking. "We need to go west, follow the slower horses." His voice carried, clear and certain, slicing through the tense morning air like a blade.

Nathan stopped in his tracks, spinning around, his expression turning dark. "What the hell are you talking about? The herd went west. We follow the damn herd."

Texas shook his head, motioning to the hoofprints in the dirt. "Not all of them did. Two horses broke off and slowed down. It could be lame, or it could be something else. But if we split here, we can cover both trails."

Nathan narrowed his eyes. "And just how the hell did you figure that out?" The words came slow, controlled, but dangerous. Then his gaze slid to Ryder.

And suddenly, everything shifted. Nathan's expression curled into something sharp. "It was him, wasn't it?" He took a step forward. "You're listening to him again?"

Texas stiffened, but he didn't answer.

Nathan let out a humorless laugh, shaking his head. "You're dumber than I thought."

The gun was out before anyone could react. Ryder didn't move, didn't blink, just stared Nathan down, his expression calm, unreadable. "You really gonna pull that trigger?"

Nathan's jaw tightened, his knuckles white around the grip of his Colt. The sun burned high above them, the heat rising off the dirt in shimmering waves. Sweat trickled down Nathan's temple, but his hands didn't shake.

Then, Texas stepped forward. "Yeah. And I trust him." His voice was low, steady. He met Nathan's glare head-on. "You got a problem with that?"

Nathan's eyes flicked between Texas and Ryder, his mouth pressing into a thin line. But he didn't fire. "You two go chasing ghosts; you're gonna get yourselves killed."

Texas didn't flinch. "The rest of you can go wherever the hell you want. Me? I'm going north." He turned and walked toward Ryder's buckskin, pulling his saddle and pack loose. Hoisting them onto his shoulder, he stepped up beside Ryder. He muttered

Wyatt Steele

under his breath, half to himself, half to Ryder. "I hope you're damned well right."

Nathan stood stiff, watching them go, his jaw clenched so tight Ryder thought his teeth might crack. Will stood beside him, arms crossed, still smirking, like a man watching a game unfold just the way he wanted. Ethan shifted uncomfortably as if he wanted to speak but didn't know whose side to take. Rourke hesitated. Then stepped back. Didn't pick a side. Didn't stop them. Just watched. Ryder didn't look back. He just tightened the straps on his pack, adjusted his gun belt, and set his sights north. It was

The climb north was slow and punishing, the weight of their saddles and packs dragging on their shoulders, each step pressing deeper into the dry, cracked earth beneath them. Ryder had no intention of weighing his horse down any further. She'd already carried more than her fair share while Nathan had played at being king. So now, he carried her saddle himself, the heavy leather cutting into his back, each step a reminder of what had been taken from him. Beside him, Texas did the same, his own gear slung across his back, his movements steady but laborious. Neither man spoke much. Not that they needed to. The only sound was the rhythmic crunch of their boots in the dirt and the distant cry of some bird circling high overhead. The sun beat down relentlessly, sending waves of heat rippling up from the dry ground, distorting the horizon in shimmering mirages. Then, after twenty minutes of trudging through dust and rock, Ryder saw it.

A ridge.

It is not just more barren land but something greener and softer. The kind of place an animal could smell before it ever saw. And suddenly, it all made sense.

"That's why they turned north," Ryder muttered, shifting the weight on his back.

Texas followed his gaze, pausing, then let out a short laugh. "Well, hell. They smelled water." He turned to Ryder, his grin wide despite the heat. "I'm glad I bet on you, cowboy."

Ryder just shook his head, adjusting his grip on his saddle. The ridge was still a ways off, maybe another hour's walk, but now they had something worth walking toward. They pressed on. By the time they reached the ridge, sweat was trickling down Ryder's back, his shirt clinging to him from the strain of the hike.

Texas dropped his saddle onto the ground with a sigh, rolling his shoulders. "Damn, I forgot how much I hated carrying this thing," he muttered, wiping his brow with the back of his wrist.

Wyatt Steele

Ryder set his own pack down with more care, reaching for his canteen. He took a long pull, the cool water rolling over his dry throat, before passing it to Texas.

The older man took a swig and let out a satisfied sigh. "Alright then, let's see where our runaways went."

Ryder knelt by the softer ground near the water's edge. The earth here was marked with prints—deep and clear—hooves sinking slightly into the dampness.

"They came through here," Ryder said, scanning the tracks.

Texas grinned. "Damn right, they did."

Then he spotted something that made his grin widen. "Son of a bitch. That's Trudy."

One of the sets of tracks belonged to a sturdy bay, and Texas didn't need a second look to know. Ryder scanned the other. A smaller set of prints, long-striding, a horse still wary, moving light on its feet. Nathan's horse.

Texas let out a bark of laughter. "When we catch up with those bastards, you riding his horse is gonna piss Nathan off something fierce."

Ryder smirked. That was true enough. But they weren't celebrating yet. They still had to catch them first. The horses were just ahead, grazing by the water's edge, the cut lead ropes still dangling from their halters. Trudy, Texas's bay, was standing calm and steady, ears flicking occasionally, content to drink from the small pool of water before lowering her head to graze again.

Nathan's horse, though, was different. It was skittish, shifting uneasily, tail flicking hard. Ryder knew that look. He stepped forward slowly, his movements careful, his eyes already reading the horse's posture. Then he saw it. A thin, bloody cut along its flank, the flies were already at it, swarming, crawling at the raw flesh.

Earning Trust

"Damn," Ryder muttered the word under his breath, his eyes locked on the wound running along the horse's flank. The gash wasn't deep, but it was raw—a jagged line where the skin had split, already darkening with dried blood. The flies had found it.

Texas let out a low whistle as he stepped closer, his brows pulling together. "Looks like when the rounds exploded, part of one clipped him."

Ryder gave a slow nod, his attention never leaving the horse. The animal was tense, muscles twitching, its ears swiveling uncertainly. It snorted, jerking back a step as Ryder took a careful step forward. But Ryder didn't rush him. Didn't push. He just lowered his hands, kept his posture loose, voice easy, steady as the desert wind.

Wyatt Steele

"Easy there, boy," Ryder murmured. "Ain't no one gonna hurt you."

The horse's ears flicked forward, watching him. Ryder moved slowly, keeping his breathing even. The animal's nostrils flared wide, taking in his scent, testing whether he was a threat. It shuffled its weight, still unsure. Ryder took another step. Then another. Closer now, he could see the flecks of sweat on the horse's coat, the way its skin trembled under the heat.

Then, Ryder reached out—slow, careful—and let the back of his fingers graze against its shoulder. The horse flinched. But it didn't bolt. Ryder held still, letting the animal get used to his touch and his presence. Then, finally, it exhaled—long, deep, the fight easing from its body. That was all Ryder needed. He let his fingers move, trailing down to the halter, gripping the cut lead rope, and giving a firm but reassuring tug.

"There you go," Ryder murmured, his voice low, soothing. He found a piece of dried apple in his pocket that he kept for his own horse and offered it to the gelding. "Ain't so bad, huh?"

The horse took the offering flicked its ears, but didn't pull away. Ryder turned, leading it slowly back toward where they'd left their saddles. By the time they reached the clearing, the horse was walking easily beside him, its breathing calmer now. Ryder tied the short lead to a low tree branch, giving the animal just enough slack to move but not enough to bolt.

Texas watched, arms crossed, an amused look in his eyes. "Damn if you don't have a way with 'em."

Ryder ignored him, already reaching into his saddlebag. His fingers found the small tin, the metal warm from the sun, the edges smooth from years of use.

Texas raised a brow. "What's that?"

Ryder popped the lid, the sharp scent of herbs and animal fat rising up from the thick, golden salve inside. He dipped two fingers into the ointment, rubbing it between his hands, warming it.

"Old Apache recipe," Ryder said simply. "Keeps the flies off. Helps it heal."

The horse shuddered beneath his touch as he gently spread the ointment over the wound, working it into the skin, careful not to press too hard. The animal shifted, tense at first—but didn't fight. Didn't try to pull away. Just stood there, watching Ryder with those big, dark eyes. Ryder kept his movements slow, patient, and deliberate. It took a minute. Then, the horse exhaled, slow and steady, its muscles finally relaxing.

Texas let out a quiet chuckle. "I'll be damned."

Ryder wiped the excess ointment on his jeans and took a step back, studying the horse's stance. "Better than dealing with people."

Texas grinned, shaking his head. "Ain't that the truth."

Once the horses were tied up and secured, the two men set about making camp. Texas got a fire going, rolling out his blanket beside it while Ryder gathered what was left of their rations. As the fire crackled, the scent of strong coffee filled the air.

Texas took the first sip, letting out a satisfied sigh. "Hot damn, I needed that."

Ryder poured himself a cup, taking a slow drink, letting the warmth settle in his chest. They sat there for a moment, the worst of the day behind them. The sun still rode high in the sky, but the worst of the heat was beginning to break, the long stretch of afternoon tilting toward the cooler edge of evening. The horses stood loose nearby, heads low, tugging lazily at the patches of grass growing near the water's edge.

Texas sat back on his heels, adjusting his hat as he glanced at Ryder. "So, what's the plan, cowboy?"

Ryder pulled a blade of grass from the ground and rolled it between his fingers, his gaze drifting toward the horizon. They had a fair few hours of daylight left. If they set out now, they might be able to catch up to the others before nightfall. Might. But if they didn't? That meant spending the night out in the open desert. No cover. No water. And right now, they had both. The small ridge provided enough shelter to keep the worst of the night winds off them. The pool of water would keep the horses settled. It wasn't much, but it was more than what they'd find out there.

Ryder exhaled slowly. "We wait."

Texas raised a brow. Ryder flicked the grass away and leaned forward, resting his arms on his knees. "Not enough daylight left. If we don't find 'em, we're stuck out there with nothing." His gaze flicked toward the grazing horses. "Here, we got water. Grazing. A place to sit and breathe. Come morning, we can move fresh."

Texas let out a sigh of relief, stretching out his back. "Glad to hear you say that. That was a long damn walk, and I ain't in the mood to do it twice in one day."

Ryder smirked. "Getting old on me?"

Texas scoffed. "Boy, I was old when you were still figuring out which way to point a gun."

Then, with a lazy grin, he reached into his pack and pulled out a bottle of whiskey.

Ryder raised an eyebrow. "Didn't know you had another."

Texas uncorked it with his teeth and took a slow swig, letting out a satisfied sigh before handing it over. "I did," he said, his grin turning a little wicked. "But I wasn't liking the company too much anymore and didn't fancy sharing it with them."

Ryder chuckled, taking the bottle.

Texas leaned back against a rock, folding his arms behind his head. "But I'll gladly share it with you."

Ryder tipped the bottle back, the whiskey burning warm down his throat. It had been a long few days. And it was going to be an even longer tomorrow. But for now? He could take a moment. Just one. The whiskey burned smooth and steady, sinking warm into Ryder's gut as he passed the bottle back to Texas. The sun had begun its slow descent, stretching long, golden shadows across the land.

Texas took another swig, letting out a slow breath as he leaned back against a rock, boots stretched out in front of him. He rolled his shoulders, working out the stiffness, and smirked. "Gunna have a few aches in the morning," he muttered.

Ryder gave him a sidelong glance, one brow raised.

Texas caught the look and huffed a short laugh. "What? You think I been behind a bar my whole life?"

Ryder took the bottle when Texas offered it back, watching him now with quiet curiosity. "You tell me."

Texas scratched at his jaw, eyes drifting toward the dying light on the horizon like he was looking at something farther back than the desert. "Used to be a marshal."

Ryder paused mid-drink, lowering the bottle slightly.

Texas grinned at the reaction. "Yeah, didn't see that one coming, did you?"

Ryder shook his head. "You don't have the look."

"Yeah, well, I used to." Texas stretched his arms behind his head. "Kirkside. West of Tucson. Rough old mining town, meaner than a coyote with its leg in a trap."

"What happened?" Ryder asked, tipping the bottle back for another sip.

Texas sighed, scratching at the side of his neck. "Got wed."

Ryder blinked. That wasn't the answer he'd been expecting.

Texas let out a chuckle, shaking his head. "Ain't always a bullet that makes a man hang up his star. Sometimes, it's just a woman, and Lila Jay is a hell of a woman," He grinned, but there was something in his eyes that said the decision hadn't been an easy one. "Didn't want her to live in a town like that," Texas continued. "Figured I'd take what money I had, move south, buy a saloon, and make an honest living. And you know what? It's been a damn good life."

Ryder smirked. "Didn't take you for the settling-down type."

Wyatt Steele

Texas gave a small shrug. "Didn't think I was either." He took the whiskey back and drank deeply.

"Still carry a gun, though," Ryder noted.

Texas grinned. "Yeah. Don't much like getting shot at, but I know how to handle myself. And folks know better than to start trouble in my saloon."

There was something comfortable about the way he said it—like a man who had earned his peace but wasn't afraid to remind folks how he got it.

Ryder nodded slowly. "So why do they call you Texas?"

Texas chuckled, shaking his head. "Now that? That's a dumb story."

Ryder smirked. "I got time."

Texas sighed, stretching out his legs. "Well, my Pa came from Texas. But I sure as hell didn't. When I was a kid, we had two Bills in my schoolhouse. The teacher got tired of calling out for the wrong Bill, so she just took to callin' me Texas Bill. And it stuck."

Ryder grinned. "So you ever been to Texas?"

Texas laughed, shaking his head. "Not once." He took another long pull from the bottle and then handed it back to Ryder. "And I don't plan on it."

Chapter 12 – The Trail Changes

The sky was still the color of deep indigo when Ryder and Texas packed up camp, their movements quick and efficient. The embers of their fire were long dead, snuffed out before dawn, leaving nothing but a faint curl of smoke rising into the morning air. Ryder cinched the last strap on his saddle, his hands moving on instinct, his mind already ahead of them focused on the trail. Beside him, Texas let out a quiet grunt as he swung up onto his bay, rolling his shoulders like the weight of the previous day hadn't quite left him. The air was still cool, the kind of crisp desert morning that never lasted long before the sun began its slow, punishing climb.

Ryder didn't wait. He nudged his horse forward, feeling the freshness in his step, the way his ears pricked toward the open land ahead. He was ready to move, and so was he.

Texas followed, his horse stepping light and sure beside them. "Well, hell, this is better," he muttered, flexing his fingers around the reins. "I don't miss that damn walk."

Wyatt Steele

They rode at a steady lope, the ground rolling beneath them, the rhythm of the horses' hooves blending with the soft morning wind. There was a sense of ease to the movement, an ease they hadn't had in days. For the first time in too long, Ryder felt ahead of the game instead of catching up. They made good time, cutting through the open desert at a brisk pace, the coolness of the morning allowing them to push forward without the heat dragging them down. It wasn't long before they reached the place where they'd split from the others.

Texas pulled up alongside Ryder, adjusting his hat as his gaze swept over the land ahead. "Didn't think we'd get here this fast," he admitted. "Makes me wonder how far ahead Rourke and the rest got."

Ryder didn't answer immediately. He was already scanning the ground, his sharp eyes tracing the faint trail left behind by the men they'd left behind. The tracks were still clear, still moving west. They hadn't stopped here long. They had kept moving.

They picked up the trail of Rourke and the others, riding side by side now, the early light stretching their shadows long across the desert floor.

Texas reached up, rubbing at his jaw, his expression thoughtful. "Think they're still trudging through this desert, or you reckon they got lucky and caught up to the herd?"

Ryder – Gone To Hell

Ryder smirked but didn't answer, his eyes fixed on the ground ahead. Something about the tracks was gnawing at him, an itch at the back of his mind that wouldn't let up.

Texas huffed a quiet laugh. "Damn, cowboy, you always this talkative in the morning?"

Still, Ryder said nothing. Because as he followed the trail, as he read the way the dust had settled, the way the prints had stretched out—he saw it.

His smirk faded. Something was wrong.

Ryder pulled back on his reins, lifting a hand. "Hold up."

Texas did the same, his brow furrowing. "What?"

Ryder didn't answer immediately. He dismounted slowly, his boots hitting the ground soft, stirring the dust as he crouched. His fingers traced the prints, his mind piecing together what had happened. Rourke and the others had kept heading west. But the horses hadn't. They had turned south.

His eyes moved in slow, careful sweeps, mapping the story laid out before him. Texas watched him closely, knowing better than to rush him.

After a long moment, Ryder exhaled through his nose and pointed ahead.

Wyatt Steele

"Nathan and the rest went that way." His hand traced the line of hoofprints, deep from the weight of men walking alongside their borrowed packhorse. Then he turned his hand slightly, pointing off to the side. "But the horses turned here. They're heading south."

Texas sat straighter in the saddle, his expression shifting. "You sure?"

Ryder stood, dusting his hands off on his jeans, and gave him a flat, deadpan look. "Damn sure."

Texas's jaw went tight. He glanced down at the prints himself as if trying to see what Ryder saw, but in the end, he didn't need to. He trusted Ryder's eyes.

He sighed, rubbing his jaw. "Well, hell. What do you make of it?"

Ryder looked out toward the southern stretch of land. The horses had veered hard, not out of panic, but with purpose. They had smelled something better than just endless dust and dry air. Ryder turned toward the horizon, already pulling the spyglass from his saddlebag.

The sun was creeping higher, dragging the heat with it, pressing against the back of Ryder's neck as he lifted the spyglass to his eye. He turned slowly, sweeping over the open land until he found what he was looking for. A rise in the land. Not much, but enough—a stretch of higher ground with deeper brush at its base. And beyond that? A darker patch. Ryder knew what that meant. "They headed toward the water," he muttered. He lowered the spyglass and turned to Texas. "What do you want to do? Follow the horses or follow the men?"

Texas didn't hesitate. "Horses."

Ryder nodded.

Texas adjusted his hat, flicking a glance back toward where Nathan's group had gone. "If they're not far, we can bring them back and take them to Rourke's group. Ain't much use to them, us two turning up on horses while they're still on foot."

Ryder smirked. "Fair point."

Texas nudged his horse forward. "Then let's ride."

Ryder didn't argue. They turned south, following the trail of the animals, riding toward the water and, if luck held, toward the advantage they needed. The land stretched wide and empty before them, nothing but heat-baked rock and brittle scrub, the wind curling dust across the open plains as Ryder and Texas rode south. The trail was clear but long, the hoofprints still fresh enough to follow without trouble. But the sun was climbing, and the heat was rising, rolling in thick and unrelenting, turning the morning's crisp air into something heavy and suffocating.

Wyatt Steele

Texas pulled at his collar, already sweating beneath the weight of the day. "They couldn't have picked somewhere closer to run off to, huh?"

Ryder didn't answer. His eyes stayed on the trail, reading the way the prints shifted, the way the dirt looked softer up ahead. The horses had slowed. And then, just over a low rise, they found them. A small clearing tucked beneath a ridge, where a shallow watering hole sat at its center. The water was low and murky, but it was water all the same, enough to draw the herd in after their long flight across the desert. The animals were spread out, drinking, tails flicking lazily at flies, their coats gleaming with sweat under the brutal light of the afternoon.

But they weren't at ease.

One of them lifted its head sharply, ears flicking, nostrils flaring. The others followed, heads turning, bodies going still. They'd spotted Ryder and Texas. And they were not in the mood to be caught.

Texas let out a low sigh, shifting his weight in the saddle. "They ain't gonna make this easy, are they?"

Ryder watched the horses carefully, the way their bodies were coiled tight like they'd bolt at the first wrong move. "Nope."

Texas rolled his shoulders. "You got a plan?"

Ryder – Gone To Hell

Ryder slid off his buckskin, his boots hitting the dirt soft, slow. Deliberate. "Same as before. Go slow, go careful. Let them think it's their idea."

Texas groaned. "Was hopin' for somethin' quicker."

But he slid down from his saddle, too, uncoiling a length of rope from his belt. The first approach sent the herd scattering, dust kicking up around them as they dodged away from the men, snorting, rearing. It took time—too much time—but Ryder had done this before. Slow steps. Low voice. No sudden movements. One by one, they worked their way in, coaxing the animals back, waiting until the herd settled again, got used to their presence. Even then, it wasn't easy. They had to rope each horse carefully and slow them down without pushing too hard, without sending them bolting again.

By the time Ryder secured the last lead rope, the sky had turned red, the sun dipping toward the horizon in a blaze of fire and shadow.

Texas ran a hand down his face, grinning despite the exhaustion. "Well, I'd say that was a hell of a lot harder than it needed to be."

Ryder smirked, coiling his rope back up. "Could've been worse."

Texas scoffed. "Yeah? How?"

Wyatt Steele

Ryder gestured toward the sky, where the first faint stars were beginning to peek through the darkening blue. "Could still be chasing 'em."

As they finished securing the horses, Texas glanced toward the horizon, then back at Ryder. "We're not reachin' Rourke tonight, are we?"

Ryder didn't even look up. He was already pulling his saddle from where they'd left it earlier, setting up a makeshift camp. "Nope."

Texas let out a heavy sigh, rubbing at the back of his neck. "Yeah, no shit."

They worked quickly, getting a small fire going and pulling out what little food they had left. The smell of coffee and burning wood filled the air, a welcome break from the long silence of the trail. Texas stretched out beside the flames, his boots crossed, his hat tipped low over his eyes.

After a long moment, he muttered, "Hope Nathan's havin' a real bad day."

Ryder smirked, taking a slow sip of coffee.

Ryder – Gone To Hell

Chapter 13 – The Price of Bad Choices

Dawn broke over the desert in soft streaks of gold and pink, the air still cool and sharp from the night. The heat had yet to sink in, but Ryder knew it wouldn't take long. By midday, the land would be an open furnace, unforgiving and dry. They moved quickly and efficiently, breaking camp without a wasted motion. Ryder tightened the last strap on his saddle, pulling the cinch firm against his buckskin's flank. She stood steady beneath him, ears pricked forward, muscles eager. No longer a beast of burden weighed down under stolen saddlebags—she was his again.

Texas was doing the same, swinging up onto his bay mare, Trudy, adjusting his hat against the coming glare of the sun. "Ain't much of a morning man, but I'll take this over another damn night out here," he muttered, stretching his back in the saddle.

Ryder didn't respond.

He was already nudging his horse forward, following the faint trail they'd left behind yesterday, tracking their way back to where they'd split from Rourke and the others. The horses moved smoothly and fast, eager to run. The miles fell away beneath them, the rhythm of hoofbeats blending with the quiet of the early morning. For the first time in days, they weren't just chasing something. They were ahead of the game.

As the sun climbed higher, the trail of Rourke's posse came into clearer focus. Ryder read the tracks like a book written in dust, his sharp gaze flicking over the signs left behind. And what he saw wasn't good. At first, the footprints were strong and steady, with deep imprints in the dirt, showing men moving with purpose and keeping pace.

Then—the pattern changed. The steps became uneven, dragging, some wider apart, some staggered. The stride lengths were shortened. A few bootprints had scuffed too deep, like a man tripping, catching himself. Ryder exhaled slowly. They were running out of water. The men had kept going, but not well.

He glanced over at Texas. "They're slowing. Running dry."

Texas wiped his sleeve across his brow, already feeling the heat creeping in. "Well, shit."

Ryder didn't reply. Something else was gnawing at him. Because if the men hadn't had water...His jaw tightened, his fingers flexing on the reins. Then his horse hadn't either.

Nathan had been leading her. He was responsible for her.

Ryder – Gone To Hell

And if that bastard had let her go thirsty—Ryder's blood boiled.

His horse moved eagerly beneath him, but Ryder barely noticed. Right now, the only thing keeping his hands off his gun was the fact that Nathan wasn't in front of him yet. But he would be. And when that time came, Ryder planned on settling some things.

The mining camp rose out of the landscape like the skeleton of a dead thing, bleached by the sun, long abandoned. A handful of crumbling wooden buildings, their roofs sagging, their walls warped by time. What was once a bustling camp of pickaxes and profit was now just dust and silence. And somewhere in that silence, Rourke and the others lay waiting. Ryder pulled his horse up, his gut already tight with what they were about to find. Texas did the same beside him, adjusting his hat and eyes scanning the scene. It didn't take long. They were there, alright.

Scattered in what little shade they could find, slumped against walls, stretched out in the dirt. Not moving much. Some not at all. Texas let out a low curse. Ryder was already swinging down from his saddle.

The heat had cooked them. Their faces were burned red, and their skin cracked, peeling from exposure. Lips dry and split.

Wyatt Steele

Their canteens were empty. The only mercy was that, at some point, water had passed through here. There were old rivulets of dried mud, a hint that a shallow stream had formed in a past storm. But these men hadn't known how to find the last traces of it. Ryder did. He took in each man's state quickly and efficiently, cataloging their condition like a man who'd seen this before. Ethan looked the worst. He was stretched out flat on his back, his lips cracked so badly they bled. His eyes barely open, staring at the sky like he wasn't really seeing it. His shirt was open, his chest rising and falling in shallow gasps.

Nathan sat slumped against a wall, arms limp at his sides. His posture was one of a man who had fought the heat—and lost. His face was coated in sweat and dust, his breaths slow and labored. Rourke was conscious, but barely. His hat had been pulled low, shading his eyes, but it hadn't done much good. His face was drawn, his mouth pressed into a tight grimace of pain. The rest weren't much better.

Texas let out a low breath, shaking his head. "Damn fools."

Ryder barely heard him. Because he saw something else. Something that sent a bolt of fury searing through his chest. His buckskin. She was still standing. Still saddled. Dust crusted thick around her muzzle. Her sides heaving. And that son of a bitch Nathan had left the weight on her back the whole damn time.

Nathan lifted his head slightly, blinking sluggishly, but he saw the look on Ryder's face. And he swallowed hard. Ryder took one step forward. Then another.

His buckskin stood there, sides shuddering, her flanks rubbed raw where the saddles they'd lashed to her had dug in too long. Nathan shifted slightly as if he wanted to sit up straighter but couldn't quite find the strength.

Ryder's voice was low, controlled—but dangerous. "You better have a good goddamn reason."

Nathan licked his cracked lips and tried to summon something—some weak excuse, some attempt at an explanation. Ryder didn't wait for it. He turned, reaching for his canteen, unscrewing the cap. He wasn't gonna waste time making a man out of Nathan just yet. First, he had a horse to take care of.

Texas, already moving, pulled out the two canteens he had left and began handing them to the men. Ryder, without a word, emptied his own water into his hat. He lifted it, holding it up to the buckskin's muzzle. She hesitated at first, still dazed, still uncertain. Then her soft nose found the water, and she drank. Not enough. Not nearly enough. But it would ease her some until he could find her more. When she was done, Ryder reached for his belt, pulling his knife from the sheath. Nathan shifted uncomfortably, his eyes flicking toward the blade. But Ryder wasn't looking at him. He took the knife in his fist and slashed through the straps, letting the saddles strapped to his horse's back and the packs fall heavily to the dirt. The buckskin exhaled a long, slow breath, her relief visible. Ryder stepped closer, running a hand lightly along her side. Raw skin. Open sores. Flies already circling. He felt his fists ball up.

Texas, still handing off the last of his water, paused, looking over. He saw Ryder's face and exhaled through his nose. "You gonna kill him?"

Ryder stared at Nathan. "Maybe."

Ryder moved through the silent ruins of the mining camp, his boots kicking up small puffs of dust as he walked. The air was still, heavy with heat, thick with the kind of exhaustion that settled into a man's bones after too long without water. But Ryder wasn't interested in the men sprawled in the shade, too weak to do much more than sip at Texas's canteens. He wasn't interested in their half-conscious mumbling, their cracked lips, or their slow-blinking eyes. He was looking for water.

A camp like this wouldn't have been built here, in the middle of nowhere, unless there had been water to sustain it. It might have dried up some over the years, but it would still be here, waiting beneath the layers of dust and time. It was just a matter of finding it. The land rose behind the camp, a gentle incline leading toward a rocky outcrop, its base littered with scrub brush and low-growing plants. The air felt different here. Thicker. Cooler. It didn't take Ryder long to spot what he was looking for.

The scrub was denser here, greener. Among the tangle of desert willow and mesquite, he saw squaw cabbage sprouting between the rocks. A plant that only grew where the soil stayed damp. Ryder crouched low, running a hand over the wind-blown sand piled against the stone. Beneath it, he felt wood. Old, but sturdy. He let out a slow breath.

"Texas!" he called, already brushing more of the grit away.

A moment later, he heard the clomp of boots on hard-packed earth.

Texas stopped beside him, hands on his hips, peering down at what Ryder had uncovered. "That what I think it is?"

"Yep." A rock-cut cistern, its opening boarded over, likely hidden beneath years of drifting sand.

Texas let out a low whistle. "Well, I'll be damned."

Wyatt Steele

They worked quickly, clearing away the sand; their boots kicked up clouds of dust as they uncovered the thick wooden planks that had been placed over the opening.

Together, they hefted the boards away, the wood splitting and groaning under their weight. The water level was low—but there was plenty. Enough to save the men. Enough to save the horses.

Ryder wiped a sleeve over his forehead, glancing at Texas. "It's got an off-channel, too." He gestured to a narrow stone trough carved from the rock. "It's blocked up, but if we clear it, it'll fill."

Texas grinned, clapping Ryder on the back. "Damn glad I rode with you, cowboy."

Ryder just grunted, already turning to the clogged run-off channel. He worked fast, scooping away the packed dirt and debris with quick, practiced movements. After a moment, a thin trickle of water began to seep through, then more, spilling over into the trough. The sound alone was enough to make a man's throat ache.

Texas turned toward the half-dead group of men back at camp. "I'll get 'em moving. They need this worse than I do." Ryder nodded, but his thoughts were elsewhere.

His horse. Ryder whistled low, a quiet, steady sound. His buckskin lifted her head, ears flicking toward him. She was exhausted, her legs stiff, but she came without hesitation, stepping carefully toward the freshly filled trough. She lowered her head, lips skimming the surface, then began to drink. Slowly. Deliberately. Ryder didn't rush her. He leaned a hip against a rock, arms crossed, watching her carefully.

She'd had a rough few days, and if he was being honest, it had been his fault for letting her out of his sight. She trusted him, and he'd left her in the hands of men who didn't deserve to lead a damn mule, let alone his horse. As she drank, Ryder reached into his coat pocket, pulling out the tin of ointment. The same one he'd used on Nathan's horse earlier. The sores on her flank were bad, rubbed raw where the saddle had pressed against her skin for too long. He moved slowly, keeping his touch light, working the thick salve gently into her coat. The horse shivered slightly beneath his hands, but she didn't flinch. She trusted him. And he wasn't about to fail her again.

Texas came back as Ryder was finishing, watching him for a moment before clearing his throat. "Hell, you take better care of that horse than you do yourself."

Ryder didn't look up. "She deserves it."

Texas snorted, kneeling to refill his own canteen.

Wyatt Steele

Ryder reached into his pocket again, pulling out a small piece of dried apple. He held it out, palm open. His buckskin's ears twitched forward. She snorted softly, then took the apple between her teeth, chewing slowly.

Ryder smirked. "You've earned it, girl."

Texas tilted his head, watching the exchange with amusement.

The buckskin turned her head and nudged his pocket. Ryder sighed, smirking, and pulled out a second piece of apple. Then, with a shake of his head, he held it out. "Just this one more; don't go asking again," he muttered.

His horse took the second apple just as eagerly as the first.

Texas laughed. "You're soft as hell, you know that?"

Ryder glanced at him, then at the group of sunburnt, dehydrated men still struggling to pull themselves toward the water. His expression hardened. "Not always."

Texas followed his gaze. His grin faded. "Guess not."

The horse finished eating, nudging Ryder's hand briefly before going back to drinking. Ryder wiped his palms against his jeans, rolling his shoulders. He'd done what he needed to do.

Ryder stood beside the water trough, arms crossed as his horse took long, slow draws of water, her ears flicking lazily as she drank. He had done what he could for her, for the men, for the horses they had recovered. And yet, something gnawed at him. His gut told him not everyone had made it. A slow scan of those gathered near the water told him who was missing.

Ethan.

Ryder exhaled through his nose, wiped the sweat from his brow, and turned away from the water. The kid was still back at camp, propped up against a splintered wooden crate. Ryder approached, taking in the way Ethan clutched a canteen with both hands—Texas's canteen. But something was wrong. The metal was tilted, the cap still off.

Ryder crouched beside him, his voice low, steady. "Kid, you get any water in you?"

Ethan blinked at him slowly, eyes sun-bleached and glassy. Then he shook his head. He opened his mouth and tried to say something, but his voice barely made a sound. Ryder felt something cold settle in his chest. His own canteen was still slung over his shoulder. Without hesitation, he uncapped it, slid an arm behind Ethan's shoulders, and helped him sit up properly. The kid was weak in his grip.

"Easy now," Ryder murmured, tilting the canteen to his lips.

Ethan drank.

At first, a few short sips. Then more.

Wyatt Steele

He coughed a little, but Ryder didn't let him rush it. He wasn't gonna let the kid choke himself trying to drink too fast. When Ethan pulled back, his breathing was shallow but steadier. Ryder watched him carefully. Something wasn't right.

Ethan was a lot worse than the others. Even Rourke, even Nathan, even Tom Calder—none of them looked this far gone. Sure, they were thirsty, but not this bad.

"Why?" Ryder asked quietly. "Why are you worse off than the rest?"

Ethan's chapped lips moved, but no sound came out. He tried again. Still nothing.

His hands twitched weakly as if he wanted to grab Ryder's sleeve and try to tell him something.

Ryder frowned, shaking his head. "Don't worry about that now. I'm gonna get you some more water."

Ethan tried to smile, but it was small, weak—a shadow of what it should be. Ryder felt that same cold feeling settle deeper. He reached for Texas's empty canteen, leaving Ethan with his, who still had some left in the bottom. "I'll be right back, kid."

Then he stood and walked away. As Ryder made his way back toward the cistern, he spotted Rourke standing near the water.

The sheriff straightened when he saw him, adjusting his hat, then took a step forward. "Grateful you came back, Ryder."

Ryder – Gone To Hell

Ryder nodded once, then began refilling the canteen. Before he could step away, Tom Calder spoke up from where he was helping one of the men drink.

"Me too, Ryder. You saved our hides."

Ryder didn't acknowledge it right away. He wasn't thinking about gratitude. He was thinking about the boy back in camp, barely strong enough to lift his own head.

"Bring up the horses," Ryder said, voice flat, business-like. "Let them drink. Then tether them in the shade."

Rourke nodded. But Ryder wasn't looking at him anymore. He was already turning, heading toward his buckskin, who stood under the scrub at the base of the incline, picking lazily at what little grazing she could find. He patted her side, feeling the warmth of her skin beneath his palm. She had been through hell. But she was strong.

"Rest easy, girl," Ryder murmured, running his fingers through her mane before stepping away. Then he headed back to Ethan.

As Ryder walked into the camp, canteen in hand, his steps slowed. Something was wrong. The first thing he saw was the canteen. The one he had left Ethan with. It lay on its side in the dirt, the cap half-buried in the dust, a small trickle of

Wyatt Steele

water soaking into the thirsty ground. A waste.

His steps slowed. Something wasn't right. He lifted his eyes to Ethan, still propped against the splintered crate where he'd left him.

Too still.

His head was tilted slightly to one side as if he'd simply drifted off to sleep. But his eyes were open. Staring at nothing. The slow burn in Ryder's gut turned to something heavier, something colder. He didn't move. Didn't breathe. The whole camp seemed to have gone silent, the usual desert sounds swallowed up in the stillness of the moment. Then, finally, he took a step forward. Then another. His boots barely made a sound as he knelt down beside the boy. For a second, he just looked at him. Ethan's face was too pale beneath the burn of the sun, lips cracked, and his body still slumped in the same exhausted way it had been before.

Ryder reached out and put his hand on Ethan's cheek; the boy's head lolled to the side, his eyes gazing at nothing. Ryder's jaw tightened, the muscles in his forearm flexing as his fingers curled into a slow, deliberate fist. This wasn't just the heat, the thirst, or the bad choices that had left the rest of them half-dead in the dust. Ethan had been trying to tell him something. Struggling to get the words out.

Now?

Ryder – Gone To Hell

Now, Ryder would never know what they were. He exhaled slowly, rubbing a hand down his face. The boy's eyes were still open, still full of the last remnants of whatever thought had been there before death took him. Ryder reached out gently, pressing his fingertips to Ethan's eyelids and sliding them closed. A kindness. But it wouldn't change what had been done. Ryder let out a long, slow breath. Then he sat back on his heels, looking down at the boy who had been too damn young to die out here.

He wasn't sure who, not yet. But someone had done this. And soon enough? Ryder was going to find out who.

Wyatt Steele

Chapter 14 - Death Brings Doubt

The heat pressed down heavily, the air thick with the scent of sunbaked dirt and sweat. Ryder still knelt beside Ethan's body, his hands resting on his thighs, staring at the spilled canteen beside the boy's lifeless form. The small trickle of water had long since vanished, the desert drinking it greedily, leaving only a darker patch of earth where it had soaked in. He had been gone for minutes. Maybe ten at most.

And yet— Ethan was dead.

A presence stirred behind him. Footsteps. Ryder didn't look up. Rourke and Will wandered back into camp, their boots kicking up the dust as they slowed near the scene before them. A hesitation.

Then Rourke's voice, careful, uncertain. "What happened?"

Ryder exhaled slowly through his nose. He rose to his feet with deliberate ease, brushing the dust from his palms, his face unreadable. "Went to get him water." His voice was flat, the words coming out measured, precise. "He was too far gone. The desert took him."

Silence.

Ryder – Gone To Hell

Then, a step forward, the creak of leather, the shifting of weight. Rourke frowned, his gaze flicking between Ryder and the dead boy. "You sure he's gone?"

Ryder finally met his eyes. And his stare was cold. No anger. No heat. Just certainty. He let the silence stretch, then spoke, his voice quiet but sharp enough to cut. "I'm sure."

Rourke hesitated. Didn't look convinced. "He didn't seem that bad earlier," he muttered, rubbing a hand over his jaw and kneeling next to Ethan, placing a hand on his shoulder and shaking the boy.

Ryder said nothing. He simply crouched again, reaching for the empty canteen, turning it over in his hand. The metal was hot from the sun, and the cap was still loose. And Ryder's gut twisted because he knew—Ethan should have been weak but not dead. He should have lived long enough to drink the water Ryder was bringing him. The desert had killed many men. But Ryder was sure the desert had killed Ethan. And that was what made the weight in his chest heavier.

"Ethan's your problem," Ryder said, his voice quiet, controlled. "I'm done helping for the day."

The words hung there, heavy. Rourke didn't answer at first, just stood there, looking down at the boy slumped against the crate, then back at Ryder. His expression twisted slightly as if he wanted to argue, wanted to push—but he didn't. Ryder turned without another word, his spurs clicking lightly against the ground as he walked away. Behind him, Rourke rose, still looking down at the dead boy, and let out a slow breath. The sheriff was rattled; that much was clear. Shaken by how fast things had fallen apart. Will had stayed quiet, standing a few paces away, arms crossed over his chest, his head tilted just slightly as he watched Ryder leave. That watchfulness set something uneasy in Ryder's spine, but he didn't turn back.

Texas was kneeling beside his saddlebags, tightening a strap, when Ryder found him. The older man didn't look up at first, focused on his task, but the moment Ryder stepped closer, Texas stilled. The shift was subtle. Instinctive. Like a man who could tell when trouble had just walked into his shadow.

Ryder didn't say anything right away; he just crouched beside him, hands resting on his knees. He let out a long, measured breath before speaking, his voice low and deliberate. "The traitor in this group has struck again. Ethan's dead."

Texas stopped what he was doing. Fully stopped. His hands went still against the worn leather strap, and for a second, he didn't move at all. Then, slowly, he exhaled through his nose. "Shit."

Ryder watched him carefully, searching his face, but Texas's expression didn't change. The two of them sat there, crouched in the dust, the camp stretching out behind them, the quiet murmur of tired voices, the occasional shuffle of boots. But here? In this moment? It was just them. Just a truth neither of them wanted to speak aloud. Whoever had killed Sam, whoever had cooked off the bullets to spook the horses, had killed Ethan, too.

Texas rubbed his jaw, his thumb running absently over the edge of his mustache, his brow furrowed deep in thought. He let out another slow breath, shaking his head. "Damn, the kid didn't deserve that."

Ryder looked back toward where Ethan's body still sat slumped against the crate, Rourke standing over him, talking in low voices with Tom and Nathan. No, the kid hadn't deserved it. But someone had made sure he wouldn't leave this desert alive. And Ryder was going to find out who.

The day dragged on, slow and thick with heat. The men barely spoke. Some sat slumped against the sunbaked walls of the abandoned mining structures, hat brims pulled low to block out the light. Others moved sluggishly, refilling their canteens from the cistern, drinking in slow, measured sips, trying not to take too much at once. The relief of water did little to mend the fractures between them. The truth was, they weren't just thirsty. They were spent. They had lost two men. Sam to a bullet. Ethan to the desert, or so they thought.

Ryder sat on the edge of a broken-down wagon, sharpening his knife with slow, deliberate strokes. The scrape of metal against whetstone was the only sound in the lull of the afternoon. The tension was thick.

It was Tom who broke the silence first. "We need to press on."

Rourke, sitting with his back to a rotting wooden beam, lifted his head, exhaustion etched deep into his face. He exhaled slowly, rubbing at his brow. "Tom—"

"Two men have died on this ride." Tom's voice was tight, edged with anger and grief. "Don't let their deaths be in vain."

A silence stretched between them. Nathan, sitting a few feet away, let out a sharp scoff. "Damn right. We came out here to put a rope around Madsen's neck. You want to tuck tail and ride home just because things got tough?"

Will, arms folded over his chest, gave a slow nod. "We lose him now; we'll never find him again."

Rourke rubbed his jaw, his fingers dragging over the stubble there. "We're in no fit state to go riding off after a gang," he muttered.

"We rest up another day," Tom said, his voice still sharp but more controlled now. "Then we ride."

For a long moment, no one spoke. Ryder kept his gaze down, the blade of his knife catching the afternoon light as he dragged the whetstone slowly across the edge.

Rourke let out a slow breath. Reluctant. Resigned. "Fine," he said at last. "One more day. Then we go after Madsen."

Tom sat back, satisfied. Nathan exchanged a glance with Will, a smug flicker in his expression. The posse had chosen their path. Rourke turned his attention to Ryder. For a second, he hesitated.

Then—"You've done enough. I'll understand if you want to leave."

Ryder paused his sharpening. Lifted his eyes. The firelight of the afternoon caught the cut of his stare, cold and sharp as the blade in his hand. He studied Rourke for a long, unmoving moment. Then he said flatly, "Do you think you'll survive without me?"

The words landed like a hammer. A slow, tense silence followed. Will let out a laugh. It wasn't a friendly one. It was the kind of laugh that held something else beneath it. Something mocking. Something

Wyatt Steele

mean. But Ryder didn't even look at him. He just turned the knife in his hand and went back to sharpening, the scrape of steel against stone cutting through the uneasy quiet. And just like that—The posse was more fractured than ever.

The heat of the day stretched on, pressing like a weight over the ruined camp. Even in the shade, the air hung heavy, thick with the smell of dust and sweat, old wood and sunbaked stone. Ryder had found himself a quiet corner, nestled beneath the broken remains of what had once been a storehouse—just enough cover to block out the worst of the sun, just enough space to stretch out and let his body sink into stillness. His hat was pulled low over his eyes, shielding him from the harsh glare of the afternoon light. For the first time in days, he allowed himself to do nothing. To let the tension bleed from his shoulders. To enjoy the simple feeling of the earth beneath him, solid and cool, the scent of distant sagebrush on the faint breeze. It was rare, this kind of peace. And it didn't last. A shadow passed over him. Bootsteps scuffed against the dry ground.
Then—
"We got a problem."
He knew the voice.
Texas.

Ryder – Gone To Hell

Ryder exhaled slowly, dragging a hand down his face before tilting his hat back just enough to glance up. Texas stood above him, arms crossed, his mouth set in a grim line.

Ryder sighed through his nose. "You always gotta be the one bringing bad news?" Texas didn't smile. Didn't joke. And that's what made Ryder push himself up, rubbing at the back of his neck. "What is it?"

Texas glanced toward the ridge beyond the camp, then back to Ryder. "I saw something," he muttered. "A flash. Up top."

Ryder's expression didn't change. Didn't need to. He already knew what Texas was getting at. Someone was signaling. And that meant trouble.

The ridgeline loomed ahead, a jagged cut of rock against the burning sky. Ryder moved silently, boots pressing firm against the dry earth, his steps careful, precise. Texas followed a few paces behind, his rifle slung over his shoulder, his jaw tight with the weight of what they were about to confirm. By the time they reached the top, Ryder slowed, scanning the empty ground. Nothing. Just dust and silence. No movement. No man waiting with a mirror in hand. But Ryder wasn't fooled.

He crouched, running his fingers lightly over the surface of the rock. The earth was disturbed, the smallest indentations breaking the natural smoothness of the dirt. Someone had been right here. Watching. Signaling. Ryder straightened, eyes narrowed against the horizon.

Texas shifted beside him, rolling his shoulders. "Well?" he asked, voice low.

Ryder didn't answer right away. Instead, he took his time, his gaze traveling the expanse of the desert beyond. His expression darkened. "Someone just gave our location away."

Texas exhaled sharply, adjusting his hat, his mouth pulling into a thin line. "Shit."

Ryder had brought his small brass spyglass with him, and he pulled it from his coat pocket. The metal was warm and worn smoothly from use. He raised it to his eye, scanning the horizon with careful, measured sweeps. Nothing. Just miles of endless land, the kind of emptiness that could fool a man into thinking he was alone.

"See anything?" Texas asked.

Ryder shook his head. Then, without lowering the spyglass, he reached into his coat pocket and pulled out a small mirror. It wasn't much—just a polished square of metal, small enough to fit in his palm. But it was enough. He angled it carefully, tilting it until the sun caught the surface. Then he flashed it. Once. Twice. Three times.

Ryder – Gone To Hell

The light flickered over the ridge, a sharp, bright glint cutting across the afternoon sky. Below, the camp was dead silent. Texas stood, arms crossed, watching Ryder with a tight expression.

The minutes stretched long. Ryder kept still, his hat pulled low, his fingers curled loosely around the mirror. He was about to lower it, about to turn back—

When it happened.

A flash.

Faint.

Distant.

But unmistakable.

Ryder snapped the spyglass back up, his pulse kicking up slightly. His gaze swept the landscape toward the source. Then he saw it. A dust plume. Rising from the desert. Coming fast. Riders.

Moving toward them.

His grip tightened around the spyglass, but his expression didn't change. He lowered it slowly, exhaling through his nose. Then he stood, turned to Texas, and met his gaze. "We're out of time."

Texas muttered something under his breath. His hands went to his belt, resting on the worn leather near his holster. Then he looked out at the desert.

At the dust. At the men who were coming. "Shit."

Wyatt Steele

And just like that—the peace of the afternoon was over.

Chapter 15 - A Dangerous Debate

The sun hung low and molten in the sky, stretching long shadows across the desert floor. The heat of the day had begun to fade, but the land still held its warmth, the ground beneath Ryder's boots radiating the last of the sun's fire. From where he stood on the ridge, he could see the dust plume rising on the horizon—growing thicker, moving with purpose. Riders.

They were coming. And they weren't coming slow.

Beside him, Texas pulled at his salt-and-pepper beard, his expression tight as he followed Ryder's gaze. He let out a breath, shifting his weight, and muttered, "We go back, tell 'em there's a snake in camp?"

Ryder didn't answer right away. His arms were crossed, his eyes narrowed the tension in his jaw sharp enough to cut. It was a good question. The kind of question that could mean the difference between a fight won, or a fight lost.

If they told the men the truth—told them one of their own had been working against them—They'd tear each other apart before the real fight even started. Ryder exhaled slowly, glancing over at Texas. "Not yet."

Texas turned his head, one brow lifting. "Not yet?"

Ryder shifted, adjusting his belt where the weight of his Colt rested, the leather worn smooth from years of use. His gaze returned to the dust cloud in the distance, watching it churn, watching it roll toward them like a slow-moving storm. "We need to fight the men coming toward us, not each other," he said finally.

Texas grunted, rubbing a hand over the back of his neck. "Fair," he allowed. "But it's gotta be one of 'em."

His tone was grim, the certainty in it sitting heavy between them. Ryder nodded once. He'd been thinking the same thing since the moment he found Ethan dead in the dust.

Texas squinted at the camp below, watching the others move in the fading light. "Not Rourke or Tom," he said, shaking his head. "I've known them too long. Neither of 'em would do this. But Nathan? He's been nothin' but a thorn in our side since the start."

Ryder glanced down at the camp as well, watching the men. Nathan stood near the remains of the trading post, arms crossed, his posture stiff, his eyes flicking toward the ridge every so often. Will stood not far from him, one boot propped on a rock, his hands resting easily on his belt.

"Nathan, maybe," Ryder admitted. "But Will? He's been watching everything too damn close."

"One of them is it then." Texas let out another slow exhale. "Then we best keep our eyes open, cowboy. 'Cause when those riders get here, the snake's gonna show its fangs."

Ryder glanced at him, expression unreadable. The wind shifted, carrying the faint scent of dust and dry sage. And in the distance, the riders kept coming. The air felt heavier now, thick with the quiet that always came before a fight. The dust cloud on the horizon was closer, no longer just a distant blur against the sky but a moving, shifting thing—riders coming hard, kicking up the desert as they rode.

Ryder and Texas stood just off the ridge now, out of sight of the others but still watching, still thinking, still deciding. Because the fight coming their way wasn't just from the men riding toward them. It was from the one standing among them.

Texas adjusted the brim of his hat, casting Ryder a glance. "You got a plan for this?"

Ryder's gaze remained on the camp below, the movements of the men. Nathan, standing rigid, arms folded. Will, leaning against a pile of rubble, looking calm, maybe too calm.

"Yeah," Ryder murmured. "We watch 'em. Both of 'em."

Texas followed his line of sight, his expression turning hard. "Nathan and Will." It wasn't a question.

Ryder gave a slow nod. "One of them's the bastard that cut the horses loose. One of them's the reason Ethan ain't breathing right now; one of them shot Sam."

Texas exhaled, his shoulders rolling slightly, tension settling deeper into them. "So, who do you want me to take?"

"Nathan," Ryder said, voice steady.

Texas's brow lifted, but he didn't argue.

"He's beat up worse than Will," Ryder went on, his mind already working through the angles. "If things turn bad, he'll be easier to control than Will."

Texas let out a long huff, shaking his head slightly. "I dunno, Ryder. That bastard's got a temper, and he's got a gun. If he doesn't like the way the wind's blowin', he'll turn on us before you can blink."

"Yeah," Ryder said, watching as Nathan moved across the camp, dragging a saddle over to the fire and dropping onto it like the last few days hadn't left him looking half-dead. "But Will's quieter."

That alone made him more dangerous. Texas scratched at his jaw, considering that. Then he sighed, rubbing a hand over his face. "Fine," he muttered. "I'll watch Nathan."

Then, he glanced sideways at Ryder, his voice going dry. "That means you're takin' Will. You sure about that?"

Ryder's answer was wordless—he reached for his Colt, flipped it open, and spun the cylinder slowly, letting the rounds catch the dimming light. Each chamber loaded. Then he snapped it shut with a quiet, firm click. "I'm sure."

Texas huffed out something close to a chuckle, shaking his head. "Hell of a thing we've ridden into."

Ryder slid the gun back into its holster and finally turned to him. "Ain't that always the way ?"

Texas chuckled again, but it didn't quite reach his eyes.

They descended the ridge in silence, boots grinding against the loose dirt and scattered rock. The wind had picked up, kicking up little swirls of dust that danced and faded into nothing. The sun was slipping lower, and the heat of the day was finally breaking—but the air still felt thick, charged with something unseen, something waiting. Ryder and Texas moved with purpose, neither speaking nor speaking;

their minds were already on the fight ahead. And the fight within. As they stepped back into the camp, the shift in energy was immediate. The men, already tired, already on edge, looked up at them. Their movements were slower and restless, the weight of the last few days hanging heavy on their shoulders.

They were worn down. The kind of exhaustion that settled into a man's bones, making him slow, making him careless. Rourke was sitting on an overturned crate near the remains of the trading post, running a whetstone over the edge of his knife in slow, thoughtful strokes. The sheriff had barely lifted his head before he caught the look on Ryder's face—something grim, something sharp.

His sharpening stilled. "Something's coming."

Ryder gave a single, steady nod. "Riders. Moving fast. And chances are, they ain't friendly."

The moment the words left his mouth, the mood shifted. Like a shot fired into the air, everyone snapped alert. Tom Calder, who had been standing near the fire, went rigid, his fingers tightening around the stock of his rifle. Nathan, perched nearby, lifted his head slowly, his expression dark. Will was already pushing off the broken remains of an old wagon, dusting off his hands like he'd been waiting for something to happen.

Ryder – Gone To Hell

Texas, standing beside Ryder, crossed his arms, watching as the men stirred like cattle, sensing a storm.

Rourke exhaled hard through his nose, set his whetstone down, and pushed to his feet. "How many?"

"At least a dozen," Ryder said, keeping his voice steady, watching everyone.

Rourke's expression barely shifted, but there was a flicker of something— calculation, strategy. "They heading straight for us?"

"Straight enough."

Tom turned fully now, his jaw tight. "Madsen?"

Ryder glanced toward the horizon, where the last of the daylight was stretching long across the land. The dust cloud was still there, rolling closer, pulling the fight with it. "We'll know soon enough."

That was all it took. The camp snapped into motion. Nathan rose to his feet, cracking his knuckles before adjusting his belt, his pistol sitting easy on his hip. His eyes flicked to Ryder once, briefly, before looking away. Will didn't say much; he just moved with deliberate ease, checking his rifle, loading shells, and his mouth quirking into something close to a smirk.

Texas leaned closer to Ryder as they stepped aside. "You tellin' me to watch

Wyatt Steele

Nathan, but I swear that bastard Will's too damn relaxed about all this."

Ryder didn't disagree. But it wasn't time for that fight. Not yet.

"Just keep your eyes open," Ryder muttered.

Texas snorted. "I'm gonna need 'em in the back of my head today."

Nearby, Rourke was already issuing orders. "We set up here. Weapons ready, ammo unpacked. Find good positions. No one stands in the open."

The men followed without complaint. They were tired, angry, broken down—but they weren't stupid. They knew what was coming.

As Ryder moved toward his own gear, checking his cartridges, he felt Texas clap a hand on his shoulder. "You be careful, cowboy."

Ryder slid the final round into place and snapped the cylinder shut with a clean, sharp click. He looked up, his eyes like steel. "Always."

And with that—

They got ready for war. The camp came alive. Gone was the sluggishness of exhaustion, the slow, trudging movements of men worn thin by heat, hunger, and loss. Now, there was purpose. The kind of energy that only came when a fight was coming.

Ryder – Gone To Hell

Rourke barked orders, his voice steady, sharp with command. "Spread out. Find cover. Keep your heads down."

Tom was already moving, striding toward the half-standing remnants of a collapsed shack, positioning himself behind it, his rifle held with quiet reverence. He checked the sights, then the ammunition and his movements were tight and controlled.

He was ready.

Nathan wasn't talking, but his hands moved with careful precision, checking his sidearm and ensuring it was fully loaded and the barrel clean. He moved with the confidence of a man who had done this before.

More than once.

He wasn't a green kid who needed hand-holding.

He was a fighter.

And that made Ryder watch him all the closer.

Then there was Will. Leaning against a stack of crates, rolling his shoulders, stretching his fingers like this was just another hand of poker. His knowing smirk hadn't faded, and that bothered Ryder more than anything else. Men about to be in a gunfight didn't smirk like that. Not unless they already knew which way the wind was blowing.

Wyatt Steele

Ryder slid his rifle from its saddle scabbard, working the lever once, the smooth mechanical click settling something inside him. He wasn't a nervous fighter. Never had been. But this? This was different. Because the biggest danger wasn't coming from the riders kicking up dust in the distance.

It was standing inside this camp. And it was only a matter of time before it struck.

Texas moved beside him, slipping his shotgun into the crook of his arm, his expression tight. Ryder leaned slightly toward him, keeping his voice low. "Keep your eyes on Nathan."

Texas gave a small nod, rolling out his shoulders. "Yeah. And you?"

Ryder's gaze flicked to Will.

The man had moved now, shifting into position near the supply crates, but not before giving Ryder a quick, measuring glance. Ryder exhaled slowly, turning his attention back to Texas. "I'll take Will."

Texas studied him for a moment, then let out a quiet, knowing breath. "You be careful, cowboy."

Ryder didn't answer right away.

Instead, he flipped open the cylinder of his Colt, checked the rounds, then snapped it shut with a clean, precise click.

His grip settled easily around the revolver, solid as stone.

Then, with a small smirk of his own, he finally met Texas's eyes.

"Always."

And then—

They waited.

The camp fell into silence. No more talking. No more muttered curses or sharp glances. Just the low, metallic sounds of men checking their weapons, the dull scrape of boots on dry earth as they shifted into position. The remains of the mining camp, long abandoned and broken by time, offered some cover but not much. Crumbling walls, half-standing shacks, and a few scattered crates. The landscape beyond wasn't any better—just an open desert, scattered rock formations, and the dry whisper of wind over sand.

It wasn't a good place for a fight. But then again, a fight wasn't asking their permission. Ryder crouched low behind the jagged remains of a stone wall, his back pressed against the crumbling rock. He wasn't alone—Texas had taken up position to his left, his shotgun cradled loose in his hands, his mouth pressed into a firm line.

Across the camp, Rourke knelt behind an overturned wagon, rifle resting against the wheel, his eyes fixed on the horizon. Tom Calder was next to him, his jaw tight, fingers curling and uncurling around the grip of his gun like he was just waiting for something to snap. Nathan had taken a spot near an old water trough, his shoulders hunched, his head down. He looked like a man bracing himself for impact.

Will was nowhere to be seen. That sent a slow, burning unease through Ryder's gut. His eyes flicked over the camp, searching—where the hell had Will gone?

Then—

A sound.

Not loud. Not sharp.

Just a faint, distant rumble. Like the earth was shaking, low and steady. The dust cloud on the horizon was closer now, stretching longer and darker, shifting and moving like a living thing. Not a mirage. Not a trick of the desert.

Riders.

And they were coming fast. Ryder could make them out now—figures taking shape in the glare of the dying sun. At least a dozen.

Texas shifted slightly, pressing his shoulder against the wall as he let out a slow, steady breath. "Hell of a welcome party."

Ryder didn't take his eyes off the dust cloud. His fingers curled around his revolver, his thumb resting on the hammer. "We knew they were coming."

Ryder – Gone To Hell

Texas exhaled through his nose, a humorless chuckle. "Yeah, well. Doesn't mean I gotta like it."

The others saw them now, too. Rourke adjusted his grip on his rifle, muttering something low under his breath. Nathan leaned forward slightly, like a man trying to gauge how much time he had left before things went bad.

And Will—where the hell was Will?

Then—

A sound cut through the desert.

Sharp. Sudden. Loud.

The first distant crack of gunfire. A bullet kicked up a burst of dust near the edge of the camp. Another shot rang out. Then another. The riders weren't waiting. They were already shooting. And just like that—The fight had come to them.

Ryder's pulse didn't quicken. He just cursed himself because he'd lost sight of his mark.

The Traitor Reveals Himself

The gunfire cracked through the dry air, sharp and unforgiving. The first bullets slammed into the ground, kicking up sprays of dust and rock as the riders closed in fast. Ryder didn't flinch, didn't panic—this wasn't his first fight.

But something was wrong.

Will.

Where the hell was Will?

Wyatt Steele

Ryder had lost sight of him just before the first shots rang out. And now, with lead flying and the camp bracing for the fight, Ryder knew he had one chance to find out before it was too late. He chanced a quick turn, shifting his weight and snapping his gaze back toward the camp. His Colt was still gripped tight in his right hand, finger light on the trigger, ready to fire if Will was where he suspected—behind him, gun raised, ready to put a bullet in his back.

But Will wasn't there.

Ryder's breath left him slow. Then his eyes caught movement up the ridge. A shadow moving against the rocks. Will. Climbing. Not toward the fight. Away from it. And just like that—Ryder knew. The traitor wasn't Nathan. Wasn't some coward looking to throw blame to save his own skin. It was Will. And he was leaving the camp to burn. Ryder's jaw tightened. His grip on the Colt flexed. The son of a bitch had played them all. Will had never planned to fight. He was getting out now, slipping away before Madsen's men closed in—so he wouldn't be caught in the crossfire. Because he wasn't on their side. He was on Madsen's.

The ridge was steep jagged, but Will moved quick, his boots finding the right footholds, his hands pulling him up like a man who had done this before. The fight was coming, but now Ryder knew the truth. And

Ryder – Gone To Hell

when this was over—He'd deal with Will Tanner. One way or another.

Wyatt Steele

Chapter 16- Bullets in the Dust

The dust rolled in thick, churning up from the pounding hooves of Madsen's riders as they bore down on the camp like a black storm cutting across the desert. The sun was sinking low, casting long shadows over the ruined trading post, the broken walls and scattered debris offering just enough cover for the men inside. But it wouldn't last. This was about to get ugly.

Ryder crouched low behind the half-fallen stone wall, his rifle steady in his hands. The air was too still. Even with the sound of the charging horses, even with the weight of the coming fight bearing down on them like a hammer, the moment before the first shot always held a strange kind of silence. A waiting. A breath before the storm hit. The outlaws were close now, too close. Still, no one fired. Not yet. The men in the camp knew better than to waste a shot. Let them come. Let them get in range. Make every bullet count. Ryder could hear the measured breathing beside him—Texas, his shotgun braced and ready, his body still as stone.

On the far side of camp, Nathan was hunched behind a pile of crates, his hands gripping his rifle so tight his knuckles had gone white. His lips curled, a muttered curse slipping past them. The hooves came closer.

Then—

A single crack split the air. Tom Calder's rifle. The first shot. One of Madsen's men jerked sideways in the saddle, his body snapping back like a ragdoll, his horse still running beneath him. He hit the ground hard, a burst of dust rising up around him, and then he didn't move. And that was all it took.

Hell broke loose.

The air exploded with gunfire. Rifles barked. Revolvers flashed. The smell of burnt powder filled the camp, the thick, acrid smoke rolling between the broken buildings like a fog. The riders didn't stop. The ones in the lead snapped their guns up, firing wildly as they charged in. Bullets slammed into the stone walls, splintered the wood of the abandoned buildings, and sent fragments of crates and glass flying. Ryder lined up a shot—and squeezed the trigger. A rider in a dark coat lurched backward in his saddle, a bloom of red spreading across his chest. He tumbled off his horse, boots dragging in the dust before his body crashed to the ground.

Still.

Texas didn't hesitate. He let one of the riders get too close—then fired.

Wyatt Steele

The shotgun boomed like thunder, the force of it lifting the outlaw clean off his horse. He hit the ground in a heap, the scatter from the blast ripping through his chest like a butcher's knife. Nathan was shouting, half-savage in his fury, emptying his revolver as fast as he was able to pull the trigger. His shots weren't always clean, but the pure force of his attack kept the riders from getting too close. Madsen's men were realizing too late—they'd expected a beaten, broken posse. A group of men ready to fold. They weren't expecting this much firepower. Bodies were hitting the ground. And for the first time—they hesitated. Ryder saw it happen. Saw the break in their momentum. And he knew they weren't going to push straight through.

The first charge had failed. Madsen's men weren't expecting this much firepower—weren't expecting a fight at all, not like this. They'd charged in expecting to gun down a bunch of half-dead men and be done with it. Instead, they'd ridden straight into a goddamn war. Madsen barked an order, his voice rising above the gunfire and the screams of wounded men. His remaining outlaws yanked their horses aside, pulling back before they were cut down completely. They dived for cover, throwing themselves behind boulders, broken walls, and anything that could stop a bullet.

And now? The fight turned dirty.

Ryder – Gone To Hell

Gone was the reckless charge—now it was a game of angles, of gunmen weaving between cover, firing blindly before ducking back. Ryder reloaded fast, keeping his head low. The air was thick with smoke, the acrid bite of it burning his throat. Somewhere to his right, Texas fired off both barrels of his shotgun, then ducked behind the splintered remnants of an old trading post wall to reload. A bullet whined past Ryder's head, slamming into the stone behind him. Chips of rock and dust stung his face.

He barely had time to curse before he heard it—

A sharp, pained grunt. Ryder's head snapped to the side just in time to see Rourke stumble back, gripping his shoulder. "Shit, I'm hit!"

It wasn't a kill shot—not deep enough, not clean enough. But it had torn a nasty gash through his shoulder, blood already seeping through his shirt.

"Stay down!" Ryder snapped.

But Rourke wasn't the kind of man to sit out a fight. He grit his teeth, grabbing his rifle with his good hand bracing it against the broken wagon beside him. He wasn't done yet. A barrage of bullets tore into the side of the wagon, punching holes through the wood and sending shards flying. Nathan and Tom were trapped behind it. Pinned down.

Wyatt Steele

Nathan's gun clicked empty. "Damn it!" he cursed, fumbling to reload.

Tom, ever steady, worked the lever on his rifle, sliding another round into place. He wasn't panicking—he was waiting for an opening. But the men on the other side weren't giving him one. Two outlaws were keeping them suppressed, rifles flashing as they sent round after round, tearing through the wreckage. Ryder moved.

Fast.

He shifted positions, ducking low, slipping between cover until he had the right angle. One of Madsen's men had just popped up to take another shot—Ryder lined him up, exhaled slowly, and squeezed the trigger. The outlaw jerked back as the bullet tore into him, his rifle falling from his lifeless hands before he crumpled face-first into the dirt. The second outlaw hesitated. That was all Tom needed. He fired once—a clean, perfect shot to the chest. The man dropped dead before he hit the ground.

Nathan let out a breath, snapping his gun shut. "About goddamn time."

But they weren't safe yet. The fight wasn't over. And Ryder knew—Madsen wasn't done with them yet. The battle had settled into a brutal, grinding exchange of fire, each side trying to pin the other down long enough to gain the advantage.

But Madsen wasn't stupid. He knew he was losing men. Knew his first charge

Ryder – Gone To Hell

had cost him more than he expected. That's why Ryder wasn't surprised when he saw movement on the ridge. Not from Will. Not this time. Madsen had sent four men up the rocky incline to the east, looking to flank them from above. If they made it to the top, the fight would be over. High ground meant death for everyone in the camp.

Ryder snapped his head toward the ridge, his instincts kicking in before his brain could even process it fully. His grip tightened on his rifle. "We got company!" he shouted.

Texas pivoted instantly, following Ryder's line of sight. He let out a sharp curse. "Shit. They make it up there, we're done."

They couldn't let that happen. Ryder didn't waste time. He dropped to a knee, shouldered his rifle, and lined up the lead man in his sights. The outlaw was moving fast, boots kicking up dust, hunched low as he scrambled for cover. He wasn't looking Ryder's way—not yet. A mistake. Ryder exhaled slowly, steady. Squeezed the trigger. The crack of the rifle cut through the battle noise. The outlaw jerked as the bullet punched into his chest, snapping him backward. He hit the ground hard, rolled once, and then lay still.

The other three froze for just a second. Long enough. Texas fired next. His shotgun roared, the buckshot tearing through the second man before he could react. The impact lifted him off his feet, his body tumbling down the rocky slope in a boneless heap.

The last two outlaws hesitated. Too long. Nathan was already moving, stepping up from his cover, his revolver snapping up with practiced ease. Two shots. Both hit their marks. One outlaw crumpled with a hard, wet thud against the rocks. The last one didn't even scream. Just slumped where he stood, blood streaking down his shirt. The ridge went silent. And just like that—Madsen's plan had failed.

Ryder didn't take his eyes off the bodies right away. He scanned the ridge, making sure there weren't more. Will was up there somewhere. Nothing.

Texas let out a low chuckle, shaking his head. "Well, that sure as hell didn't go how he planned."

Nathan was breathing hard, still keyed up, his jaw clenched. He holstered his revolver with a sharp snap. "Bastard should've sent more men."

Ryder didn't reply.

He wasn't looking at the ridge anymore.

He was looking at Madsen.

The outlaw leader had seen exactly what happened. And now, for the first time, he looked uncertain. His men were dead. His flank was gone. And Ryder could tell, just from the way he tightened his grip on his reins, that Madsen was starting to reconsider. They weren't an easy kill. This wasn't the slaughter he expected.

And that?

That meant Ryder had just turned the tide of the fight.

The battle had settled into a brutal rhythm—gunfire, smoke, shouts of warning, the sharp crack of bullets hitting stone. The once-quiet trading post was now a war zone, thick with dust and the acrid scent of gunpowder. The sun was sinking, casting the landscape in deep, blood-colored light, stretching long shadows over the dead and the dying. Madsen's men weren't backing off. Not yet. But Ryder could feel it. A shift. There was hesitation in their charge, the slight delay before a man moved from cover, and the frantic way they fired now—not with confidence, but with desperation.

They were starting to realize they were losing. But that didn't mean they were done. The crack of a rifle split the air, followed by the sharp snap of a bullet ricocheting off the wooden beams near Ryder's head. He ducked low, reloading fast, peering through the thinning smoke. Another outlaw broke cover and charged. Not with a gun. With a knife. And he was headed straight for Texas. Texas had just fired both barrels, his shotgun empty as he worked to reload—he didn't see the bastard coming.

"Texas!" Ryder barked.

Texas turned just in time. The outlaw was already on him, blade flashing in the dim light. But Texas was quicker than he looked. Instead of scrambling for his gun, he shifted his weight, gripping the shotgun by the barrels and swinging it like a club.

Crack.

The butt of the shotgun slammed into the outlaw's skull hard enough that Ryder heard the sickening crunch of bone giving way. The man stumbled, the knife slipping from his fingers as he crumpled onto his back, eyes blank, body twitching once before going still.

Texas stood over him, shotgun still raised. He exhaled slowly, then muttered, "Dumb bastard."

But there was no time to rest. Gunfire still filled the air. Ryder turned, scanning the battlefield, tracking the movement in the dust and smoke. Nathan was firing like a man possessed—but then, suddenly, his revolver clicked empty. He snarled in frustration. No time to reload. Without hesitation, he lunged for a rifle lying near the body of a fallen outlaw. He barely looked at it, just snapped it up, cocked the lever, and kept firing.

Ryder – Gone To Hell

Madsen's men were starting to break. Ryder saw it in the way they moved now—hurried, frantic men looking for an escape rather than a kill. He shifted his rifle, tracking movement. Madsen himself was just beyond the fight, watching.

Madsen's fingers tightened on his reins. His eyes scanned the battlefield, watching another one of his outlaws drop to the dirt. He was losing his nerve.

The gunfight didn't end all at once. It was a slow, crumbling collapse. Ryder could feel it in the way Madsen's men faltered, the rhythm of their shots breaking apart. Could see it in the way some of them started backing toward their horses, guns still drawn but no longer firing with purpose. They were breaking. Ryder shifted his rifle, sighting along the barrel, tracking one of the last men still holding his ground.

A tall bastard with a dark coat and a steady hand. Madsen's best shot. A man Ryder had seen drop one of Rourke's men back in Wells Crossing. A killer. Not anymore. Ryder exhaled slowly, lined up his sights, and pulled the trigger. The crack of the rifle rang out over the battlefield.

The outlaw's head snapped back, blood misting the air before he crumpled into the dirt.

And that?

Wyatt Steele

That was the breaking point.

The remaining outlaws turned tail, scrambling for their horses. A few grabbed their wounded, dragging them up into saddles. Others just ran, sprinting through the dust for whatever cover they could find. Madsen stayed a moment longer. He sat in the saddle, his face unreadable as he watched his men scatter, their bodies left behind in the bloodstained dirt. Then, slowly, his gaze lifted—locking onto Ryder.

A silent promise.

A warning.

This wasn't over.

Not by a long damn shot. Ryder didn't move. Didn't blink. He just held Madsen's gaze, cold as iron. And then, without a word, Madsen wheeled his horse around, spurred it hard, and rode off into the distance, dust rising in his wake.

The dust was still settling. Gunpowder hung thick in the air, sharp and acrid, mixing with the heavy scent of blood. The trading post looked like it had been through hell—bullet holes punched through wood and stone, shattered glass glinting in the dirt, bodies scattered like broken toys. Seven outlaws dead.

The rest? Gone.

Ryder lowered his rifle, rolling his shoulders, feeling the ache set in now that the adrenaline was bleeding away. A low groan came from the side—Rourke, still leaning against the wagon, his shirt dark with blood. Ryder turned, eyeing the wound. A graze, but deep enough to keep the sheriff hurting for a while.

"You gonna live?" Ryder asked.

Rourke let out a rough chuckle, grimacing as he shifted. "Ain't the first time I've been shot."

Ryder gave a slow nod. "Hope you didn't like that shirt."

Rourke huffed but didn't answer.

Nathan stood near one of the wrecked buildings, breathing hard, dust and sweat streaking his face. He looked around, eyes scanning the battlefield like he couldn't quite believe he was still standing. Tom leaned against the broken wagon, reloading slow, steady, like his hands weren't even shaking.

And Texas?

Texas turned to Ryder, exhaling slowly, tipping his hat back with one hand.

"Well, cowboy," he muttered, voice dry. "Reckon, that's what they call a good day's work."

Ryder didn't answer right away. His eyes were still on the fading dust trail where Madsen had disappeared. Then he looked up at the ridge. Will.

Wyatt Steele

Chapter 17 – Into Hell

The battle had ended, but the rage inside Ryder hadn't cooled. The air still hung thick with the acrid stink of gunpowder, the dirt still soaked in blood. Seven of Madsen's men lay dead, their bodies cooling in the dust. The rest had ridden hard for the horizon, kicking up a long plume of dirt as they fled. But Ryder wasn't watching them anymore. He was watching the ridge. Will Tanner had vanished just before the first shot rang out, slipping away like a coyote sensing the shift of the wind. Ryder had lost sight of him in the chaos, but he knew exactly what the bastard was up to.

Running.

Texas was reloading beside him, his shotgun still warm from the fight, sweat beading along his brow beneath the wide brim of his hat. He turned slightly when he caught Ryder's gaze, his expression dark with knowing.

Ryder pulled a breath through his teeth, exhaling slowly, his voice flat as iron. "You go tell them about Will." He holstered his revolver and adjusted his rifle's sling. "I'm gonna finish him."

Texas didn't argue. Didn't even ask if Ryder was sure. He just gave a slow, grim nod, snapped the barrel of his shotgun shut, and turned toward the camp. That was the good thing about Texas. He understood. Some things had to be finished. Ryder didn't waste another second. His boots pounded against the dry ground as he took off up the ridge, moving fast but carefully. The land was rough, scattered with loose shale and jagged rock. The kind of place a man could slip if he wasn't paying attention. But Ryder's focus wasn't on the ground. It was on the trail ahead. The wind had picked up, swirling the dust where a fresh set of boot prints cut through the ridge's loose dirt. They were deep, hurried—Will was moving fast. And that told Ryder two things. One, Will knew he'd been found out. And two? He wasn't just running. He was heading for the horses. Trying to get to Madsen before Ryder got to him.

Ryder's jaw clenched.

Not today.

The sun was dipping lower, casting the land in long shadows, the sky a bruised mix of orange and blue. The ridge gave him a view of the camp below—Texas was already talking to Rourke and the others. Ryder turned back, his pulse steady, his steps quick. The prints were fresh. Will wasn't far. Ryder could smell the bastard's sweat in the wind. A low growl rumbled in his chest. Will hadn't just betrayed them.

Wyatt Steele

He'd played them. He'd shot Sam in the face. Blown half his skull off just to stir the pot. He'd spooked the horses and left them stranded in the desert. He'd killed Ethan out, stolen his water, and made the kid too weak to fight back. And then? Then he'd murdered him—just to silence his confession.

All of it. For Madsen. For a man who didn't give a damn whether he lived or died. Ryder's grip tightened around the rifle as he rounded a bend in the ridge. And there he was. Will Tanner. Running. Ryder watched him for a moment. Watched the way he ducked low, glanced over his shoulder, scurried like a rat toward the horses waiting below.

Will was running hard, his boots kicking up loose shale, his breath ragged in the dry heat. The ridge sloped downward toward the horses below, their silhouettes dark against the fading light. The sun was sliding toward the horizon, stretching his shadow long ahead of him—a dark, slinking thing fleeing toward escape.

He knew that Ryder was somewhere behind him, gaining.

His hands shook, cursing under his breath. His fingers were slick with sweat, the leather sticking against his skin as he adjusted the holster at his hip. He had to reach the horses. Had to get the hell out of here. If he could just make it down the slope, just mount up and ride—A sound.

A sharp crunch of rock behind him. Will's breath hitched. He whipped his head around, eyes wide, searching the ridge.

Nothing.

No movement.

But he knew Ryder was there. He could feel it. The way the air felt heavier, pressing down on him. The way his heartbeat hammered against his ribs, too fast, too wild. Will picked up speed, stumbling over the uneven ground, nearly pitching forward. His boot slipped on a loose stone, and he barely caught himself, throwing a hand against the dirt to keep from tumbling down the slope.

And then—

A voice.

Low. Steady.

"You look like hell, Will."

Will froze.

The words sent ice through his spine, locking his joints and setting every nerve on fire. He turned slowly, his chest rising and falling in shallow, panicked breaths. And there he was.

Ryder.

Standing dead still twenty yards back, rifle in hand, its barrel angled downward in an easy grip. He wasn't rushing. Wasn't even breathing hard. Just watching. Like a wolf that had already decided how this was gonna end. Will swallowed hard, his throat dry as dust. His eyes flicked toward the horses again—so close now. If he could just—

Ryder lifted the rifle.
Not pointed. Not yet.
But close enough.
Will stilled, his muscles tight.
This was it. His cover was blown. His story was over. But maybe... maybe there was still a way to turn this around. A slow, greasy smile spread across Will's face. He let out a breath, hands raised, palms out. "Damn, Ryder. You sure know how to make a man feel unwelcome."

Ryder didn't smile. Didn't even blink. Will's grin faltered just a little. He licked his lips, stalling for time. His mind was moving fast, grasping for a way out. Talk your way clear. Make him hesitate. Will let out a slow, easy chuckle.

"Now, I get it," he said, voice smooth, keeping his hands up. "You think I've been playing you. That I set this whole thing up. That I'm the one who—"

"Save it."
The rifle didn't waver.
Will's pulse hammered.
Ryder knew.
He knew everything.
Will's hands curled into loose fists at his sides. His mind raced, weighing his

options. He still had his gun. If he could just get to it fast enough—

Ryder cocked the rifle. A smooth, deliberate sound in the dry air. Will's grin vanished. That's when he knew. Knew he wasn't gonna talk his way out of this. Knew that if he moved wrong, Ryder would put a bullet in him before he ever cleared leather.

And that?

That was a problem.

Will kept his hands up, his fingers splayed, sweat beading along his brow. The smirk was there—too forced, too thin. He licked his lips, eyes flicking toward the ridge's edge, toward the scattered brush below where his escape route had once been. But Ryder had cut him off, and now there was no running.

Will let out a breath, shaking his head with a chuckle. "Guess you caught me, huh?"

Ryder said nothing.

Didn't blink.

Didn't move.

Just stood there, rifle steady, gaze cold as a winter wind.

Will's grin wavered. His hands itched for the gun at his hip, but Ryder's trigger finger was too still, too calm. He knew if he made a move too soon, he'd be dead before he cleared leather.

So instead?

Wyatt Steele

He talked.

Tried to keep his voice even, light, like none of this meant a damn thing. "Alright, fine." He sighed, rolling his shoulders, buying time. "You want the whole story? You got it." He lifted his chin, his smirk settling back into place. "Sam? I shot him right in the head. Blew his face clean off. Just to see how it looked. There wasn't much left, to be honest. Damn shame."

He watched Ryder.
Nothing.
No reaction. No flicker of emotion.
So he went on.

"Spooking the horses? That was easy." He gave a small shrug. "Set a little fire, tossed some bullets in, and let the heat do the rest. You ever hear a round cook off? Hell of a sound, I'll tell you." He chuckled, but it fell flat against the silence.

Ryder's stare was razor-sharp as if he were looking through him, not at him. Will shifted his weight slightly. His fingers twitched. He needed Ryder to look away, just for a second. So he saved the best for last. His smirk widened, cruel now.

"Ethan?" He let out a slow whistle. "Now that was fun."

Ryder's jaw tightened, just barely.
Will saw it.
And so he pushed further.

"Kid was easy. Too weak to fight. I told him—give me his water, or I'd put a knife in his ribs. He did. Handed it right over, no argument." He leaned forward slightly, voice dropping. "And then? I held my hand over his mouth. Just for a minute. Maybe less. Didn't even try to fight me. Just let himself go." Will grinned. "Quietest killing I've ever done."

And that's when he saw it. A flicker. Not much—but just enough. A shift in Ryder's stance. A tightening around his shoulders. And his eyes. They didn't just go cold. They burned. Like a furnace door had been thrown open. Will knew that look. Knew it in men who had already decided. If he didn't make a move now, he wasn't walking out of this.

Will drew.

Or at least, he tried.

His fingers barely brushed the grip of his gun before—

BOOM.

A gunshot ripped through the air.

A scream followed. Will's revolver spun through the dust, landing somewhere in the rocks behind him. His right hand was a ruin, fingers curled inward, blood spilling between them as he staggered backward, a howl of agony ripping from his throat. He clutched his wrist, dropping to his knees, breath coming in ragged gasps. Sweat, pain, and fear twisted across his face. "Jesus Christ, Ryder—!"

Wyatt Steele

"Get up." The words were ice.

Will's head snapped up. Ryder stood there, rifle lowered now, but his other hand rested on the revolver at his hip. Waiting.

Will's breathing hitched. He was bleeding bad, the pain rolling over him in waves, his fingers slick with his own blood.

This was it.

He wasn't getting out of this alive.

Not unless he talked fast.

His mouth opened—

"I said get up." Ryder took a slow step forward.

Will swallowed hard, his stomach twisting.

The gunshot was one thing.

But the look in Ryder's eyes? That was worse. He knew what men looked like before they killed someone. And Ryder? Ryder wasn't hesitating.

He pushed up, stumbling as he got to his feet, swaying slightly. Blood dripped onto the dirt, leaving a trail behind him.

Ryder grabbed him by the collar and shoved him forward. "Walk."

Will staggered ahead, breath ragged, pain pulsing in his fingers.

Behind him?

He could hear Ryder's footsteps. Unhurried. Calm. Steady. Like a man who'd already decided this walk would end at a grave. And for the first time in his miserable life— Will Tanner was terrified.

Ryder – Gone To Hell

Rourke stood with his arms crossed, his jaw clenched tight enough to crack the stone. Nathan was pacing like a caged animal, fingers flexing near the grip of his revolver, his face dark with fury. Tom Calder? He didn't pace. He didn't move. He just stood there, dead still, staring at the blood-soaked traitor being marched into the firelight.

Texas had already told them everything.

And now?

Now, Will Tanner had to face what he'd done.

Ryder shoved him forward, sending him staggering into the dirt. The blood from his ruined hand left a trail behind him, dripping slow and steady, pooling at his feet when he landed hard on his knees.

But Will? Will laughed.

The sound was ragged, breathless, half-strangled from pain—but it was laughter all the same. He tilted his head back, grinning through the agony, through the sweat sticking his hair to his forehead.

"Goddamn, boys. That was a hell of a ride, wasn't it?" He coughed, his shoulders shaking. "And you never saw it coming." No one spoke. Will's smirk widened. He looked at Rourke first. "You're a goddamn fool," he said, shaking his head. "Too soft, too trusting. That's why your men died. That's why they'll keep dying." Then to Nathan. "Big, bad Army scout. Thought you were better than me? Thought you were smarter? Guess not."

Nathan took a step forward. Texas caught his arm, holding him back.

Will just kept grinning. Then his eyes flicked to Tom. "Ethan was an idiot," he spat. "Weak. He had no business out here. I did him a favor."

Tom's jaw tightened. Will leaned back slightly, lifting his uninjured hand and wiping the sweat from his forehead. Then he met Ryder's gaze. "Guess that makes you the biggest fool of all, huh, Ryder?" His voice was hoarse, but the amusement was still there. "All those years riding alone, and you still thought you could trust people."

He grinned again. "I played you all like a goddamn fiddle."

And with that, he turned back to Rourke, leaned in close, and— He laughed. Right in his face.

Then—

BOOM.

Will's laughter cut off instantly. His body jerked sharply as the bullet tore through his skull. For a split second, his grin stayed—like he hadn't quite registered that he was dead yet. Then his legs buckled. His body crumpled to the dirt, face-first. Blood pooled beneath him, seeping into the dust, into the ground, into the boots of the men he'd betrayed.

Silence.

Smoke curled from Tom Calder's revolver.

No one moved.

No one breathed.

Tom let out a slow exhale.

Then, at last, he spoke. "That was for Ethan."

No one argued. No one said a damn thing. Because, for once, justice had been served.

Wyatt Steele

Chapter 18 – The Showdown

The dust hadn't settled. Not really.

It hung in the dry desert air, swirling around Will Tanner's body, mixing with the blood that seeped into the dirt. The wind picked up, sending grit against the boots of the men standing in a rough circle, staring at the corpse-like it might still have something left to say. But Will was done talking. Rourke exhaled slowly, rubbing at his temple, his exhaustion plain. The fight, the betrayal, the loss—it was too much. His shoulder was still bleeding from the grazing wound he'd taken in the battle, but he wasn't paying it any mind.

He looked up, scanning the faces of the men left standing, then spoke, voice heavy with finality. "We've lost too many. We should head back."

The words landed like lead.

Nathan scoffed, shaking his head. His face was streaked with sweat and dirt, his clothes torn, his movements stiff from exhaustion. But the fire hadn't gone out in his eyes. "No. Hell no." He took a step forward, boots grinding into the dirt. "Madsen's still out there. We leave now, and

Ryder – Gone To Hell

we might as well have dug Sam and Ethan's graves ourselves."

Silence stretched.

Tom Calder hadn't moved. He was still staring at Will's lifeless body, his expression unreadable. Then, finally, he spoke." Madsen won't stop." His voice was rough, edged with something dark. "He'll find more men, come back stronger. And next time, he won't run. He'll burn everything down. Kill anyone who gets in his way." His fingers curled into fists. "I ain't going back while he's still breathing."

Ryder listened, saying nothing. The wind rattled against the skeletal remains of the trading post, a loose board creaking in protest. Texas shifted his weight, crossing his arms, watching Ryder with that knowing look. He was waiting. They all were. Finally, Ryder broke his silence. He looked at Texas, his expression unreadable. "You still got another bottle of whiskey in that pack?"

Texas arched a brow, the corner of his mouth twitching. "Why? You thinkin' about celebrating?"

Ryder pulled off his hat, ran a hand through his sweat-matted hair, and then shook his head. "No." He slid his hat back on, glancing toward the horizon, where the last of the sun was bleeding out behind the mountains. "I'm thinkin' I might need a drink after this."

Wyatt Steele

A slow, knowing smirk pulled at Texas' mouth. He reached into his saddlebag and pulled out a bottle, holding it up. "Then you're in luck, cowboy."

He tossed it over. Ryder caught it without looking.

Rourke let out a sharp breath and shook his head. "We ride at dawn."

Dawn crept over the horizon, casting long, ragged shadows across the rugged landscape. The air was crisp, carrying the scent of sagebrush and the promise of a relentless sun to come. Ryder tightened the cinch on his saddle, his movements deliberate, each tug and buckle a ritual that steadied his mind for the hunt ahead. Rourke approached, his face drawn, the lines of fatigue etched deeply into his features. His shoulder was hastily bandaged, the bloodstain a stark reminder of the battle they'd just survived.

"You sure about this?" Rourke's voice was rough, carrying the weight of unspoken fears.

Ryder met his gaze, eyes cold and unyielding. "Madsen's out there, makin' for the border. We let him cross into Mexico; we'll never see him again."

Tom Calder stepped forward, his rifle resting on his shoulder, eyes hard. "Then let's make sure he doesn't."

Ryder – Gone To Hell

Nathan, limping slightly but with a fire in his eyes, nodded. "Bastard's got a reckoning comin'.

Texas handed Ryder a canteen, his usual smirk replaced by a grim line. "Let's ride, cowboy."

They mounted up, the horses sensing the tension, hooves pawing at the ground, eager to move. With a silent nod, Ryder spurred his horse forward, leading the posse into the vast expanse of the desert, the sun rising at their backs. The trail was fresh, tracks clear in the soft earth, leading southward toward the border. Ryder rode ahead, eyes scanning the horizon, every sense attuned to the signs around him. The others followed in a loose formation, weapons ready, eyes sharp.

Hours passed, the sun climbing higher, the heat becoming oppressive. They rode in silence, the only sound the rhythmic thud of hooves and the occasional call of a distant hawk. Ryder raised a hand, bringing the group to a halt. He dismounted, crouching beside the trail, fingers brushing against the disturbed earth.

"What is it?" Rourke asked, dismounting and approaching.

Ryder pointed to the ground. "Two sets of tracks here, off the main trail. Looks like they veered off in a hurry."

Wyatt Steele

They followed the tracks a short distance, coming upon a grisly scene. Two bodies lay sprawled in the dirt, gunshot wounds evident, their lifeless eyes staring up at the unforgiving sun.

"Madsen's men," Tom muttered, nudging one of the bodies with his boot.

"Looks like his own men turned against him after the failed shootout at the mining camp," Nathan said, his voice tight with anger. "He must've shot them to keep control."

Ryder stood, jaw clenched. "Means he's only got maybe two or three left with him now. A desperate man with nothin' left to lose is the most dangerous kind."

They remounted, urgency driving them forward, the trail leading them toward a looming formation in the distance—Dead Man's Bluff. The sun was dipping low in the sky when they reached the outskirts of the bluff. Sheer rock walls rose up, casting long shadows across the canyon floor. The trail narrowed, hemmed in by jagged rocks and thorny brush.

Ryder signaled for the group to halt. "This is it. He's cornered."

"No way out but through us," Texas said, checking his revolver.

"Let's finish this," Rourke growled, pain and determination etched into his features.

Ryder – Gone To Hell

They advanced cautiously, weapons ready, eyes scanning every shadow. The air was thick with tension, the silence oppressive. As they rounded a bend, the canyon opened up into a wide clearing. There, near the base of the bluff, Madsen and his remaining men had made a final stand, their horses tethered nearby, eyes wild with fear.

Madsen stepped forward, a twisted grin on his face, eyes gleaming with a manic light. "Well, well. Looks like the end of the line."

"It is for you," Ryder replied coldly, leveling his rifle.

The two groups faced off, the weight of their shared history hanging heavy in the air. The sun cast the canyon into shadow as the final confrontation loomed. The sun cast an orange glow over Dead Man's Bluff. Shadows stretched long across the canyon floor as Ryder and his men approached, their horses' hooves stirring up small clouds of dust. The air was thick with tension, every creak of leather and jingle of spurs amplifying the silence.

Madsen stood in the open, flanked by his last two men. His eyes gleamed with a manic light, a twisted grin spreading across his face as he watched them approach. He raised his revolver in a mock salute. "Took you long enough," he sneered.

Wyatt Steele

Rourke nudged his horse forward, rifle steady in his hands. "No more running, Madsen. You know how this ends."

Madsen's grin widened. "Oh, I do. But I ain't going alone."

The world seemed to hold its breath. Then, as if a dam had burst, gunfire erupted. Nathan cried out as a bullet tore through his leg, sending him sprawling behind a boulder. Tom and Texas reacted instantly, their guns blazing. Madsen's men barely had time to aim before they were cut down, collapsing into the dust. A shot rang out, and Rourke staggered, clutching his side where a crimson stain spread rapidly. He gritted his teeth, refusing to fall.

Amidst the chaos, Ryder and Madsen locked eyes. Time seemed to slow, the sounds of battle fading into the background. They stood, guns drawn, two predators circling, each waiting for the other to make a move.

"This is where it ends, Madsen," Ryder said, his voice cold and steady.

Madsen chuckled darkly. "Maybe for you."

In a blur, both men fired. The crack of gunshots echoed through the canyon. Ryder felt a searing pain graze his arm, but he held his ground. Madsen, however, stumbled, a look of shock crossing his face as blood blossomed on his chest.

Ryder – Gone To Hell

He dropped to his knees, coughing, blood staining his lips. "Guess... I was wrong," he gasped.

Ryder approached cautiously, gun still trained on the dying man. "You brought this on yourself."

Madsen tried to laugh, but it turned into a wet, choking sound. "Maybe so... but at least... I made you work for it." With that, he collapsed, the light fading from his eyes.

The canyon fell silent, the acrid smell of gunpowder hanging in the air. Ryder lowered his gun, the weight of the moment settling over him. He turned to his men.

"It's over," he said quietly.

Rourke nodded, pressing a hand to his wound. "About damn time."

Wyatt Steele

EPILOGUE

The acrid scent of burning flesh and wood filled the air as the flames consumed the bodies. No graves were dug, no markers placed—just ash carried away by the wind, erasing the last traces of Madsen and his men.

Nathan sat on a nearby rock, pressing a bloodied cloth to his wounded leg. His face was pale, but his eyes remained sharp, locking with Ryder's in a moment of unspoken understanding—a grudging respect forged in the fires of battle. Tom stood apart from the group, his gaze lost in the distance, thoughts hidden behind a stoic facade. Rourke, weary and bleeding from a gash along his ribs, broke the silence. "It's done," he muttered, voice heavy with exhaustion.

Texas approached Ryder, a faint smile tugging at his lips as he extended a flask. "You were right, cowboy. I do need a drink."

Ryder accepted the flask, taking a long swig before handing it back. The burn of the whiskey was a welcome distraction from the lingering pain and loss. Mounting their horses, the men began the journey back to Wells Crossing. The rhythmic clatter of hooves against the hard-packed earth was

Ryder – Gone To Hell

the only sound, a somber accompaniment to their thoughts.

As they rode into town, the first light of dawn painted the sky in hues of pink and gold. The saloon's doors swung open, and Lila Jay rushed out, her face a mixture of relief and concern.

"You boys look like hell," she exclaimed, ushering them inside. "Sit down. I'll get you some food and the best whiskey we've got."

The saloon was quiet at this hour, and the usual rowdy patrons were not yet stirring. Lila fussed over them, bringing plates of steaming stew and glasses filled with amber liquid. Ryder and Texas settled at a corner table, the weight of recent events hanging heavily between them.

After a long silence, Ryder spoke, his voice low. "I'll stay in Wells Crossing only long enough for my horse to heal. Then I'm leaving before you find me something else dangerous to do."

Texas chuckled, the sound rough but genuine. "Whenever you're passing through, there's a room, a meal, and the best whiskey in the territory waiting for you."

Ryder nodded, a faint smile touching his lips. They raised their glasses in a silent toast, the clink of glass a small but significant acknowledgment of battles fought and friendships forged.

Wyatt Steele

As the sun continued its ascent, bathing the town in warm light, the men ate in companionable silence, each lost in their own thoughts yet united by shared experiences. The promise of rest and the familiarity of routine awaited them, but the scars—both seen and unseen—would remain, reminders of the price paid on the rugged trails of the frontier.

THE END

Next in the series – Ryder – Hell To Pay

A Note from the Author – Your Review Matters

If you've enjoyed this book, I'd love to hear your thoughts. Reviews are invaluable—they help other readers discover the story and allow me to continue bringing history to life through fiction. Whether it's a few words or a detailed review, every bit of feedback is greatly appreciated.

Thank you for riding along with me on this journey. I hope you've enjoyed it as much as I have.

If you have a moment, please consider leaving a review. Your support means the world.

ALSO BY WYATT STEELE

TRAIL OF THE GUNFIGHTER SERIES

VENDETTA RIDE – THE WRATH OF WYATT EARP

THE OUTLAW McCOY SERIES

DRIFTER GRITTY WESTERN SERIES

Printed in Dunstable, United Kingdom